Co..... .....n't change a word. If your next book is half as good as Coyote Stands, you should give up your day job.

—H L, Florida

Talk about a page turner. I absolutely refused to put it down until the end.

—K W, Arizona

Duane's "A Rookie's Guide to" books set the standard for pool table maintenance and repair, so I jumped at the chance to read Coyote Stands. I'm glad I did.

—J B, Arizona

I had an opportunity to read Duane's first novel "Last Chance" and loved it. "Coyote Stands" builds on that and is even better. I can't wait for Duane's third novel.

—C W, Indianapolis

Holly Forkner disappears while riding her horse alone.

Upland, Arizona Chief of Police Troy Forkner, Holly's husband, scours the wilderness of northern Arizona, first by air then on the ground, looking for her.

Officer Nina Miller believes the perpetrator had an accomplice who may be hiding Holly in a motor home at the Upland reservoir.

Nina's partner, Rookie Officer Pike Tso, a Navajo Indian, believes Navajo spirits or skinwalkers may have abducted Holly.

Sheriff's Deputy Thomas Justman takes advantage of the situation by sending a ransom note and implicating a loner Indian in Holly's disappearance.

Meanwhile, J.C. Forkner, Troy's brother, is involved in a pool game using his wife, Blondie, as the wager.

Also by Mose Duane

A Rookies Guide to:

Pool Table Maintenance and Repair

Buying and Selling a Pool Table

Playing Winning Pool

Pool Table Assembly

Novels:

Last Chance

Coyote Stands

Coming soon:

Drugs and murder keeps the Upland officers on their toes.

Available

All of Mose Duane's books are available on Amazon.com, Kindle, b&n.com, phxbilliards.com, and all major books sellers through Books-in-Print.

About the Author

Mose Duane was awarded Writer's Digest 2000 National Self-Published Book Awards' certificate of merit for The Billiard Guidebook. He has written four *A Rookie's Guide to* billiard books, and two novels, *Last Chance* and *Coyote Stands*. He is currently working on his third novel.

Like him on Facebook.com/MoseDuane.

COYOTE

STANDS

Mose Duane

Phoenix Billiards, Glendale, AZ

www.phxbilliards.com

This novel is a work of fiction. Names, characters, places, and incidents are the product of the author's imagination or used fictitiously. Any resemblance to actual persons—living or dead—business establishments, events, cities or locales is wholly coincidental.

ISBN   978-1505580952

Authors Note

This is a book of fiction. The characters and places, although vaguely set in Northern Arizona, are figments of my imagination. Also, I have taken great fictional liberties with some Navajos' viewpoints toward skinwalkers, (shape changers), and Witchery Way spells, callings, and other beliefs.

Enjoy

Mose Duane

Coyote is a trickster.
Coyote waits in the dark to frighten.
But when Coyote stands, he is pure evil.
—Early Navajo adage

1

Holly Garcia Forkner loved the Northern Arizona forest this time of year and this time of day. The long and bitter winter was well past, and summer, with its warm and pleasant afternoons, was finally breaking away from spring. Holly loved riding her beige filly, Chance, at a steady gallop through the woods in the afternoon warmth, wind whistling in her ears and blurring her vision with colorful summer trees and wild flowers. Frolicking in such a manner cleared her mind and made her feel free. It gave her time to think about being stuck forever in a small town, about being tied down to a man who spent more time as a cop than a husband, and about having a baby son who seemed to consume all of her time.

She now understood how her mother had felt when she'd complained about being "saddled with a kid," day in and day out. Holly's mother—whose Bible-thumping father (Holly's grandfather) had forced her into a marriage she had neither been ready for nor wanted—had never been a family person, nor a loving, devoted wife or mother. Holly had promised herself that she would never end up like that. But now, here she was with a family she was neither ready for nor wanted. Did she still love her husband? Did she ever? How about her son? Those were questions she'd asked herself a thousand times. She felt something, of course. But was it love? Whatever that meant, she wasn't sure she had any idea anymore. But the one thing she did know was she'd grown bored of the small town, back woods life of Upland, Arizona. She felt her youth was passing her by just as it did her now old, haggard, and worn-out mother, who had spent her entire life in a small town outside of Butte, Montana and had never known anything else.

Lost in her thoughts, Holly gave Chance free rein through the forest as usual, and the horse was galloping along with ease. Chance knew the way home and always stayed on the rutted trail until they reached that part of the Verde River that ran east to west. From there, she would turn east, follow the rippling water for a mile or so then loop around making a grand circle back through the woods, and head for home, without direction from Holly. But just as Holly was anticipating the turn along the river, a large coyote swiftly overtook them, and then darted across their path. Chance broke her stride so abruptly that Holly had to catch herself with the saddle horn to keep from falling.

"Easy, girl," Holly said and gave the horse a reassuring pat on the neck. "We've seen coyotes before."

Chance's ears perked up, she neighed softly, and came to a complete stop. Holly looked around, turning one way in her saddle, then the other, trying to see anything that might be back in the murky woods or down by the clamorous river. "I think he's gone," she said. But the horse neighed again and took a step backward. "Did you hear something else?" Holly asked. "Hello, is someone there?"

But all seemed quiet, maybe too quiet. She could hear the river but oddly no birds were singing their summertime warbles, a sound Holly always looked forward to. She then heard a sound that surprised her. It was heavy breathing, as if someone had been running, and it came from a thicket of scrubby trees, in front and left of her, and very close.

"Hello," Holly said again, her voice feeling weak. A shiver ran down her spine. She'd been on this trail a hundred times and rarely saw anyone. Maybe a friendly fisherman at the river bank, usually someone she knew, but nothing more and even that was rare.

Then, with a sudden rustling of branches, a hefty, dark-skinned Indian emerged from the thicket so quickly that it startled her. He was not a modern Indian in the usual cowboy garb they wore today, but one that looked like a warrior from a hundred years ago. Horizontal zigzagging streaks of white and black paint could not hide a conspicuous, slightly crooked, nose. His head sat solidly atop a hulking muscular frame and neck. He had long hair held in place with a hooded cape made of the head and back of a coyote pelt, ears and tail still attached. He wore only a large hanging leaf like a loincloth, held in place around a lean stomach by a leather cord. Dead ground-squirrels, rats, and mice—each tethered by its hind legs—dangled from the cord. A large sheathed knife, its handle fashioned from the head of a rattlesnake, also hung at his side. Holly saw all that in an instant.

3

That the leaf did not hide his substantial endowment did not escape her notice either. Holly felt uncomfortable and ashamed for noticing, considering the circumstance, but there it was, hanging long and loose.

And yet, somehow the Indian looked vaguely familiar. "Do I know you?" Holly asked, sounding a little hopeful but more nervous than she'd wanted.

Suddenly the Indian moved forward, shoved his hands above his head and screamed. Chance reared and Holly rolled backward, tumbling off her saddle. She hit the ground with a bone-jarring thud.

The Indian loomed above her. His head tilted one way, then the other, appearing mesmerized as she scrambled to her feet.

Holly's long, black hair cascaded around her neck, over one shoulder, and stopped at the middle of her heaving breasts. Her round and sun-darkened face glowed and her immense brown eyes glistened.

When she turned to run, the Indian was instantly in front of her.

"Ta-ay?" the Indian uttered in a low voice, more of a question than a statement.

"Do I know you?" Holly asked again, trying not to show fear.

"Ta-ay!" He reached for her face. A smile stretched the limits of his black and white face, and showed dull but healthy teeth.

"What the hell are you doing?" Holly jerked away. "Do you know who I am? I'm the wife of the Upland police chief."

In an instant, the Indian had his knife in his hand, the fangs on the snake handle gleaming. Then, without hesitation, he thrust the knife forward. The ten-inch blade penetrated her trousers just below her groin, and then sliced diagonally upward and out.

She fell to her knees, grasping herself.

The Indian kicked, his foot caught her in the temple and she folded to the ground.

2

Upland, Arizona's Greyhound bus terminal was a converted gas station on Palm Street, on the town square's north side. Tony "J.C." Forkner stood in front of the vending machines at the station drinking bottled water and chewing a mouthful of gum when his wife, Blondie, arrived on the only bus of the day. J.C. was clean shaven, wearing matched pants and sport shirt, with shined shoes and matching belt. He was tall and lean.

"Wow!" Blondie said when she spotted him.

J.C. bowed and smiled broadly. "I hoped you'd notice the new me."

"How could I miss?"

"Haven't had a smoke or drink in over a year . . . water and chewing gum is about it, maybe a soda pop now and then."

"I'm impressed." Blondie smiled.

"That's half the battle," J.C. said and winked at her.

Blondie had left South Bend, Indiana—home of the world-famous Fighting Irish of Notre Dame—three days earlier with barely enough money for the bus ticket. Two years ago, with delusions of something greater than a much older husband holding her back, she'd run away with a good-looking, fast-talking pool hustler called Rabbit for the big time up in Chicago. They never made it. She and Rabbit had managed to survive for most of those two years hustling pool in small out-of-the-way honkytonks in southern Indiana and Illinois. Finally, growing weary of him and tired of living in the cheapest, bug-infested motels they could find, she'd grabbed enough cash for the bus ticket and slipped away while he slept. She'd taken the money from his stash, money he refused to spend on rent or food because he'd put it aside for pool, so they'd have enough to hustle one more big game, he'd told her. Sure, they could win, or more precisely, she could win, but then he would manage to lose it just as fast trying to prove he was the best but always finding someone just a little better than him. That was the way it had gone for months: win some, lose more, but never winning enough to take them to the big time.

She'd planned on returning to California to stay with her parents, but when she found out her son was living in Arizona, she'd shortened her trip, swallowed what pride she had left and called J.C. It was as if she'd never been gone, or she'd simply been on vacation. He never asked about "that worthless hippie" Rabbit. He asked only about how she was, how her pool-playing abilities were progressing, and if she'd made her dreams come true, and so on. She'd left him many times in the past and he'd always treated her as if she still belonged, as if she'd never left.

"You look ten years younger," she said.

"It's the good country living, and trying to set an example for the boy, is my reasoning. But you look great, too."

Petite Blondie was twenty years younger than J.C. and looked it; though overly thin with rumpled cropped hair she didn't feel it. "Don't lie to me," she answered. "I'm dog tired, pig hungry, and look like crap."

"Crap-looking is in the eye of the beholder. To me, you look fine, though a little meat on the bones wouldn't hurt. So, what do you say if we go home and stuff ourselves and maybe get some rest?"

"Tony, I'm only here to see Kid," she said. "Don't make this hard."

J.C. held his hands up in submission. "I know, I know, I didn't mean anything. You just look hungry and tired, is all, and Kid and I live in the apartment above the saloon. We can at least go there and get some grub . . . got any bags?"

Blondie raised a medium-sized tote bag and smiled. "This is it."

J.C. carried the bag for her, and opened the door.

"Always the gentleman."

"You're still my wife and as long as you're here, you'll be treated as such."

3

Holly's husband, Upland's acting police chief Troy Forkner, leaned back in one of several wooden chairs on the back porch of their house, wearing blue jeans and no shirt, his bare feet perched up on the wooden railing. He clutched a bottle of Bud Light. Their two-year-old son, Jesse, also scantily dressed in only a diaper, sat beside Troy on the deck of the porch. He was as busy as ever running a toy train around a circular plastic track that encompassed him.

Half an hour earlier, Troy had watched Holly put her horse, Chance, through her paces. Both were as sharp as ever, even better at their routine than the day they'd won the Upland Rodeo Beauty Queen Pageant a couple of years back. He'd watched with admiration and delight as they rode in harmony around barrels and over jumps. Holly was still as beautiful as ever in her thin ruffled blouse, tight khaki slacks, matching vest, and sequined Corral boots. She'd gained a few pounds carrying Jesse but had not let it settle in one spot. Somehow she'd managed to stay well proportioned and the beauty and grace of her and Chance together never ceased to amaze or excite him. And often, as she had today, she would let

Chance break out, gracefully sail over the top board of the corral fence, and head for the national forest that enclosed the south boundaries of their property. Troy had paid close attention as Holly's ravishing round behind bobbed sensually a few inches above the saddle as the horse cleared the fence by a large margin. Loose, racing into the woods like the independent woman she wanted to be, Holly could be gone for an hour or more.

But Troy didn't mind. In fact, he loved it when Holly disappeared on her riding excursions. She always came back energized, full of life and vigor, and horny as hell. Troy never understood the connection, but never questioned the results either, and always smiled broadly when Chance broke for the fence.

The corral sat a few yards behind the house among what used to be ten acres of trees. Troy, in an attempt to make Holly happy, had cut more of them down than he'd originally wanted to make room for her horse barn, corral, and riding arena. "A happy wife is a happy life;" his mother had told him more than once during the several coming-of-age conversations they'd had when he was a teenager. To his knowledge, though, she had never married and therefore had no real understanding as to what a wife, happy or otherwise, might have been. She'd owned and operated the Last Chance saloon before bequeathing it to Troy's older brother, J.C., and had done an admirable job raising her two sons while doing so. There, she'd mixed with the rowdies of her time and bore J.C. and Troy. Neither brother had any idea who their fathers were or had been; only that they were different men and both had vanished. A fate Troy would never subject his own boy to, he vowed. He knew being a cop had its dangers at times but figured he'd always be around for his own son and wife.

But Holly was not happy, and Troy knew it. She seemed depressed, preoccupied, and short tempered most of the time. It wasn't always obvious, never anything he could put a finger directly on, but more of a subtle shift in her mannerism. Troy couldn't figure it out to save his soul and now maybe his marriage. He loved her and was sure she still loved him. But something was wrong.

If only he had more time, if only he didn't have to work so much, maybe he could figure it out. Now, added to his normal cop duties was overseeing the construction of the new police station the town was finally getting around to building. He was simply too busy for anything that even resembled a normal family life.

But today would be different, he told himself. He'd actually taken the afternoon off to watch Jesse while Holly went on her ride, and was anxiously anticipating her return. It would be a reconciliation of sorts, he told himself. He would convince her of his love. "It's going to be a beautiful afternoon," he said somewhat excited to his son and took a sip of his brew when he saw the horse appear from the woods. But when he realized Chance was alone, he leaped to his feet. "What the hell?" Holly was much too good of a rider to have fallen, and even if that were the case, she wouldn't have let Chance come home without her, unless she was hurt. He leaped the porch railing and bolted to the horse. "Where's Holly?" he asked, but knew full well he wouldn't like the answer even if the horse could actually tell him. But Chance reared, raised high and pumped her front hooves, settled to the ground and headed back toward the woods, stopped, turned, and raced back to Troy.

Troy grabbed Jesse and managed to mount the horse with the baby in his arms. Holly's saddle was much too small for him, but he clumsily held on as Chance, in full gallop, headed back into the woods. Twenty minutes later they stopped just before reaching the river. Chance had stopped in the same spot she'd stopped earlier, but Holly was nowhere in sight.

"Holly," Troy called several times, trying to raise his voice above the wail of the baby. The only response he got was a few bird trills and flutters. He slid off the horse and found where Holly had fallen and, from there, a trail of broken grass and branches that led to the river. On the groundcover along the trail he also found splotches of fresh blood.

He followed the trail to the river and made several trips up and down the bank, hopeful that maybe she'd crawled to water and he would find her there, waiting for him among the river vegetation and debris. But the trail ended at the river's edge, and he found nothing more.

4

Forty feet of ragged cliffs banked the north side of the sweeping curve of the river that had etched its way through the national forest for a thousand years. Natural openings that dotted the cliff's face, washed out of the sandy rampart by the years of erosion, were once home of the Zuni and Aztec, and later the Apache and Navajo. The largest of these natural caves lay at river level in the cliff's face but some distance from the water's rocky edge. Time had concealed it with shrubbery, boulders, and piles of driftwood.

Holly lay in front of the cave, but it was the trees high above the cliff's jagged face that she was looking at when she awoke. The wind pulled strong and continuously through the trees, sounding to her like a thousand ancient souls speaking to her at once, but nothing she could understand.

She was alone, lying face up on the rocks at the river's edge, her hands tied behind her back and her ankles bound tight around her boots. She attempted to move, to free herself, but the pain from river rocks jabbing into her back and bindings digging into her wrist hindered her. She settled down and again listened to the wind in the trees. What was it saying? "Nothing," she told herself, trying to be rational. "It's only the wind." Then she screamed, loud and clear, "Where the fuck are you?"

And, suddenly, as if the wind itself had blown him in, the Indian stood beside her, his gnarly, frightful face peering down at her. He was no longer wearing the coyote skin, only the yucca leaf.

"Who the hell are you?" she yelled. "What do you want with me?"

The Indian kicked her in the ribs.

"You motherfucker," Holly screamed as she recoiled in pain.

The Indian pulled back to kick again and Holly rolled onto her side away from him.

He grunted some meaningless word, untied the leather cord he used for a belt, let it drop to the ground, and stood exposed, large and loose.

Holly grimaced, said nothing, and did not move.

Then, awkwardly, as if he wasn't used to walking, he turned and staggered across the rocks to the river and leaped into the brisk water. Dogpaddling, he swam halfway across the river, turned in a sweeping circle, and swam back, as if refreshing himself. When he came out of the river he was on all fours and, looking more like dog than man, shook the water from himself. But when he stood, he stood tall and lean, though his face was still grotesquely streaked black over white.

Holly watched him approach and when he stood over her with his legs spread, his genitals hanging above her, she screamed, loud and clear, "Get the fuck away from me." She recoiled and both feet came up kicking.

He dodged her strike. Then his foot caught her solidly in the rib-cage. She rolled sideways and folded in pain so severe she nearly passed out.

"You son of bitch," she cried, and could not control the tears.

He snatched her by the cords around her ankles, brutally dragged her inside the cave, and tossed her onto the dirt at the back wall. When she moaned loudly, he kicked again, but this time only hard enough to keep her silent.

He retrieved his belt of fetid rodents, and removed the fattest one. Unsheathing his knife, he showed it to her and smiled. Her blood dulled the shine of the blade, and he deliberately did not clean it. Instead, he decapitated and skinned the rodent, placed it on a small, flat board, and carefully sliced it into narrow strips, allowing her blood to mix with the slices. One of the strips, long and round like a fat earthworm, he slid into his mouth, rolled it around his tongue, and sucked out the juices. Then, slowly, he chewed the meat and swallowed it in small bits. He savored it, as if it were more than food, as if it were part of her, consumed more for pleasure than sustenance.

Wide-eyed, she watched, breathing heavily, but otherwise not moving or speaking. She did not dare.

He held up a second slice of raw rodent and carefully rubbed it over his knife. He raised his head and, bird like, slowly slid the morsel past his lips and again savored the juices of the combined meat and human blood before chewing and swallowing. He continued his

Mose Duane

ritualistic exercise until he'd consumed all the remaining cuts then, with a satisfying smile, he flashed the knife at her. It was clean, bright, and void of her blood.

She tried to be strong and confident without provoking another kick. "What do you want with me?" She said and, as much as she tried to avoid it, she could not take her eyes from his long, dangling genitals that hung just above the dirt.

He ignored her and skinned the remainder of the rodents, sliced them into slivers and laid them out to dry at the back of the cave.

That done, he crouched low beside her, "You Indian," he said, "pure like me."

She shook her head from side to side. "No, I'm not."

"You Ta-ay," he yelled, and with a flick of his knife, he cut the cord binding her boots, forced her legs apart, and squatted between them.

She tried to scramble away but when the blade instantly touched her throat she settled.

He slid his fingers up her legs, first one side then the other, but stopped at her injured thigh, the injury he had inflicted earlier. Her blood had congealed and covered that part of her trousers. He leaned in close and smelled the blood, then smelled her crotch.

Holly closed her eyes and did not resist.

He left the cave for a minute then came back with a handful of water and, with his bare hands, washed the dried blood from the wound. It was superficial, clearly and cleanly slicing only the inside of her left thigh. As he worked, he could not take his eyes from her legs where her trousers pulled tight into her crotch. She watched his

16

eyes as he worked. He seemed gentle. He seemed distracted.

She brought her foot up and wildly kicked. Her boot caught him on the chin and sent him scrambling backwards. She came up on her knees. But, faster than a heartbeat, faster than she could see or perceive, he was on top of her with a backhand to her head so severe that she flew backward onto an outcropping of rock. He drew back for another punch but, mercifully, stopped.

"You Ta-ay, my woman," he said and retied her ankles. Then he quickly left the cave, securing the entrance with a large boulder, which he rolled into place with ease.

5

Late that afternoon, Upland police officer Nina Miller and rookie officer Pike Tso left the construction site of the new police station. Nina had been with the department for four years and, at twenty-five, was still the youngest officer on the force; even the rookie Pike had a year or two on her. Thin, with long, dark, curly hair and dark skin, Nina was the only daughter of one of the two African-American families who lived in Upland, and the only offspring of those families to stay in town, and then become a police officer, which she did over the objections of her parents. Pike was Navajo Indian, handsomely tall, with a straight prominent nose, neatly cropped hair, and russet skin. Troy had hired him only a couple of weeks earlier.

The department had been working out of the temporary doublewide trailer for well over twenty years and Nina was happy to see the new station finally coming together. She had always felt that the new facilities would not only make the department appear more professional and efficient, it would also attract more much-needed recruits like Pike.

During construction, Nina had taken it upon herself to oversee the installation of the communication equipment on top of her regular duties. Then Troy had assigned the rookie to her for a week. Both those tasks, being more than she'd bargained for, had sapped her energy. She fully intended on taking the evening off, starting with stopping by the Last Chance saloon to have a quick beer with Troy and maybe his brother J.C. before driving home for some much needed rest.

Nina turned her small, old Ford patrol car south on Rawhide Street and eagerly headed away from the commotion of the construction and toward the old station to drop off Pike when her nose began to twitch. She rubbed it. Her nose always twitched when she felt something wasn't right. The car hit a pothole, bounced twice, and she instinctively ducked. Nina was relatively tall for a female, a quarter inch or so south of six feet, and even with the seat all the way back her knees banged the steering wheel and her head struck the headliner every time the car hit a substantial bump. She held onto the steering wheel with both hands in case it was another flat tire or something worse. Nina had questioned anyone with authority who would listen as to why she should settle for some crappy, cramped patrol car purchased back when the town was trying to economize, but got no logical explanation.

The radio suddenly crackled, first with static, then: "Nina, you there?" It was Officer Duke Brock, the oldest head on the hierarchical totem pole at the station. She was sure he'd been around since even before she was born. A thin, wiry man in his mid-sixties who wore large bifocals that made his face appear even thinner, he was an ornery old cuss that Nina admired greatly.

The antiquated radio was the only communications device onboard her patrol car and any call sounded like a 1930's Philco. The car had no computer, not even a hookup, which made all the latest equipment at the new station a waste for Nina. She picked up the radio mike, held it close to her face, and keyed it. Unlike a telephone, the old mike had to be keyed to talk and then released to listen. "I'm here, Duke, what's up?" Proper radio protocol required an "over" when she wanted to listen and an "out" when she was done talking. Another annoyance she couldn't understand given today's technology, though no one at the station really adhered to the procedure anymore.

The radio crackled again. "Troy just called in. It appears that Holly rode her horse off into the woods, down by the river behind Troy's house, and didn't come home with it."

"Damn," Nina said and unconsciously rubbed at her nose. "Did Troy find her?"

"Not yet. He found where she fell and some blood but not her."

"Blood, Christ. How long ago?"

"Just got the call, but don't know for sure when it happened. This morning maybe, maybe this afternoon . . . and no one else is available, so I called you."

"Me, you, and Troy," Nina said, "seems like we're always on duty."

"Joe and the new guy, Pike," Duke said.

"Yeah, right," Nina said. "Joe's never around and the rookie's probably worthless—" she looked at Pike and smiled "—anyway, the three of us are more than we need as far as I'm concerned. We can handle it, and I'm on the way." Nina released the mike button.

Troy was the ranking patrolman and acting chief when Nina joined the force, and she'd fallen for him hard. He was white and country, and quick with a smile, but he was more than cute to Nina. He was Handsome with a capitol H, and when he'd asked her out she was weak-kneed and petrified at the same time. She could honestly say it was love at first sight and something that could have become so serious. But, at that time, her parents had thought it unseemly that she would be dating a superior and put pressure on her to call off the affair. Back then, they still had a great deal of influence over her and were already disappointed in her for not finishing college and even more disappointed when she decided to stay in Upland to become a "common" police officer. So she called it off with Troy and regretted it ever since. That was four years ago and she hadn't had a serious relationship since. Sure, she'd dated a couple of times, a grad student from Flagstaff a year or so ago, the town's lawyer more recently, but it quickly became apparent to her that she wasn't really interested in either of them, not with Troy still around.

In the meantime, Holly had come into Troy's life and robbed Nina of any possible reconciliation with him. And now Holly was missing . . . Nina liked Holly okay, but still . . . maybe . . . her heart skipped a beat and she shunned the thought. Now that's mixed emotions with a capitol M, she thought.

Nina flipped on the roof flashers and siren, eased the patrol car into a wide U-turn, accelerated west on Mesquite Street, and out of town. Considering its age and puny size, the automobile performed flawlessly as she pushed the accelerator pedal to the floor. But it quickly maxed out at 80 miles per hour.

"Do you know where you're going?" Pike asked.
"Been there."

Pike made sure his seatbelt was tight and held on. "I see the old Ford still has some pep," he said.

"Piece of crap," Nina muttered.

6

    Upland's town square lay dead in the middle of town. It had originally been set aside for the county courthouse, but when rejected as the county seat, the town designated it a park. Small businesses ran amuck with brick and wooden structures of varying sizes and shapes on the opposite sides of the streets that encompassed the square. Earlier, J.C. had taken his time going to the bus station by walking around the square, visiting shop owners and employees he knew, which was most of them. It still amazed him how friendly and cordial the folks of Upland were. Now, however, with Blondie "dog tired and pig hungry," at his side, he cut through the park, the shortest and most direct route to the Last Chance saloon.

    Bright green leaves swirled high in the trees, squirrels skittered from limb to limb, birds courted in their sing-song voice, and kids of all ages romped about. All brought out by a warm sunny afternoon.

    "This is nice," Blondie said.

    "Kid loves it here."

    "And you?"

"Well, to be honest, this is home. The only thing missing is you."

"Tony!"

"Okay, okay. I'll behave. But that's how I feel." He paused and when she did not respond, "Come on, the saloon is just on the other side of the street." He headed across at mid-block. Cars going in both directions stopped to allow him passage and the drivers lightly tooted their horns, smiled, and waved him across.

"How do you rate?" Blondie asked.

"Hey, what can I say? The whole town loves me," he answered as he smiled and waved back, calling many of them by name.

Inside, the saloon was warm and pleasantly lit by neon beer fixtures and other low-intensity lighting. It smelled mildly of booze and burgers and was half-full of patrons sitting at tables and booths. A few loners were perched on wooden stools at the bar, and all seemed to be talking at once.

"At one time," J.C. said as he opened the door for Blondie, "the roughneck miners considered this place as the gateway to the wilderness, the last place to stop for libations before tackling the wilderness. That's how it got its name, you know."

"I would have bet on it," Blondie said laughing. "I can tell you're pretty proud of it."

"Yeah, and nowadays it's overrun by tourists, boaters, campers, and bikers up from the hot flatlands."

"Nice," Blondie said.

"Have a seat." J.C. pointed at an empty stool at the end of the bar.

Dana Excel was behind the bar filling in as bartender in J.C.'s absence, as she did more often than not. Dana wore her usual tight leather pants, sleeveless blouse, and biker vest. She was of average height but taller than Blondie, a little chunky, had a tattoo of the universe orbiting her left arm, and sported a long reddish braided ponytail tied off with a Harley pendant that rubbed her rear end when she moved. The pendant represented the Harley Davidson Low Rider that will forever be her only means of transportation.

J.C. introduced the woman to each other.

"Beautiful," Dana said and winked an approving eye at Blondie. "J.C. told me about you, how pretty you were and all, but I never believed he'd be so lucky."

Blondie squirmed uncomfortably but smiled.

"Not to worry," J.C. said as he strolled around the bar and, remembering what she liked popped open a bottle of Coors Light and set it in front of her, "she's got a boyfriend named Hog, she's not hitting on you."

Blondie held up the bottle, took a sip, but kept an eye on Dana while looking around the room. The long walnut bar, along with a matching ornate back-bar behind it, dominated the right side. A mix of two and four-top tables with high-back walnut chairs took up the middle, and a row of upholstered booths lined the back wall. It all looked homey and inviting, though somewhat noisy.

"During the early years of Upland," J.C. said, "the town square was surrounded by twenty or thirty such establishments, but they were all destroyed by fire some time ago. This place was among the five saloons rebuilt along the south side of Mesquite Avenue, directly across from the town square. Mother inherited it when I was still in short pants and suspenders, and then gave it to me when she died."

"I remember the story," Blondie said. "But you lost it in a pool game before we met."

"Right you are, but what you might not know is that a couple of years ago, Kid won it back from Hog, Dana's boyfriend, in another pool game."

"Wow," Blondie said with a low whistle. "He's that good?"

"Gonna be a world beater."

"Where is he? I can hardly wait."

"He'll be here soon. Remember, he doesn't know you're coming."

"How is he?"

"He's grown a little," J.C. said as he disappeared into the small kitchen behind the back bar. "In the meantime, dinner's on me," He tied on an apron, turned up the gas grill, and began his preparations.

Blondie watched through the serving window with amusement, her stomach rumbling. "What's cooking?" she asked.

"My specialty, J.C. burgers and sweet potato fries."

"Smells wonderful," she said. "I'm glad things turned out well for you guys after I left, I was so worried about him, you know, the way I dumped him on you and all—"

At that moment, the back door opened, flooding light into the room, and Blondie looked up.

"Something's burning," Kid said as he wandered through the door. "Dad must be cooking again."

"Junior?" Blondie said, "Look at you, I wasn't expecting to see an almost grown young man.

"Mom!" Kid yelled and ran to her.

After several minutes of hugging and kissing and crying, J.C. fixed enough food for the three of them and they sat at a booth reminiscing while eating.

When Blondie couldn't contain her yawn any longer, J.C. explained that the upstairs apartment had only two bedrooms and that Kid would have to sleep on the couch for a while, and Blondie could have his bed.

"That would be great," Blondie said in agreement. "I'd like to spend at least a couple of days with him."

"No way," Kid quickly said. "You guys are my dad and mom, and you should sleep in the same room."

"Can't argue with that logic," J.C. said and smiled.

Blondie smiled too. "I'll take the couch. You guys can keep your beds. Anything would be better than the bus."

Upstairs, the apartment was spotless with all new wall-to-wall carpet, new furniture and appliances, and a fresh coat of taupe paint on the walls, trimmed in white.

"This is nice," Blondie said. "Very, very nice."

"Dad had it fixed up so you'd stay when you came home," Kid said.

"I called him three days ago. He did all this in three days?"

"He's been working on it for months," Kid said beaming. "He said you'd be home someday."

"Come on, son. Give me a chance to talk to her before you go blurting out such things."

Blondie looked at J.C. "After what I did, you'd really let me stay, just like that?"

"In a heartbeat," he answered. "In a heartbeat."

7

Low and bright, the sun burnt through cirrus clouds in spectacular amethyst colors, as officer Nina Miller and her new shadow, rookie Pike Tso, holding on for dear life in the passenger's seat, sped south and out of town following Highway 89. Though traveling much too fast for road conditions, Nina knew the route well, every hump, bump, and curve, and kept the car stable enough. Then, just prior to the steel-truss Verde River Bridge, she swerved right in a long sweeping turn that included cutting off the corner by several yards, and hit the rutty trail along the north bank of the river at breakneck speed.

"This is not the Indy 500, Danica," Pike said. "What's the hurry?"

"I don't know. I'm worried about Troy. I want to get down there and back before it gets too late in case we need to form a search party. There are always fishermen around and I want to make sure they don't screw things up, or leave before I can talk to them."

"Okay, okay, I get it," Pike said holding on. "But we have to get there in one piece."

Normally, on any ordinary day, Nina loved the forests of northern Arizona. She loved the mountains, lakes, and streams that surround and passed through Upland and the Coconino National Forest. She was born and raised here, graduated from Upland High School and attended Northern Arizona University in Flagstaff for a couple of years before joining the police force. Back when she was a rookie, she had taken full advantage of any opportunity to patrol the town's southern boundaries, which put her only a couple of miles from the river that circled south of Troy's property, where it abutted the national forest that surrounded most of Upland. As a child, she and her father had spent many weekend afternoons there trying to "snag the big one" with just a pole, a short line, and a hook. And later, she and Troy had spent many hours there sweating to the to and fro of the river. But today the forest provided no goodwill. Though she knew the river trail and the spot where Holly had disappeared, the four miles getting there with her head banging the headliner every time the miserably undersized car bottomed out, was no picnic.

To make matters worse, she expected to be alone once she got there, not see two Navajo County Sheriff's pickup trucks already there, sitting exactly where they shouldn't be. Two men were standing beside one of the trucks watching her small white patrol car bounce up the rugged trail toward them. A trail they had just traversed in the two Chevy 4-by-4 pickups. Nina recognized both men.

"How's it possible for those two assholes to be here already?" Nina asked Pike as if he would know. She rubbed her ever-twitching nose.

"Sheriff's deputies Naize and Justman," Pike said. "I met both of them a couple of days ago."

Coyote Stands

Deputy Naize, a squat Hopi Indian whom Nina only knew by his last name and deputy Thomas Justman who had been a sheriff's deputy for as long as she could remember and who, according to the general hubbub, blew most of his pay in the casino poker rooms, stood waiting. Justman was a big burly white man who claimed to be part Havasupai or Hualapai, Nina couldn't remember which, and strove to look the part with a perpetual tan, from a tanning booth she guessed. There was also a turquoise and silver bracelet dangling low on his right wrist, and a small "medicine pouch" hanging on a turquoise and silver chain around his neck for all to see. He was dressed in a rumpled uniform and aviator's sunglasses, though the sun had already dropped well behind the treetops. She had no use for him.

"What the hell are you doing here, *Thomas*?" Nina said, knowing full well that he preferred his last name over his first, thinking it sounded more native. She was peering through the open window of her cruiser as she pulled alongside his truck.

"Look who it is," Justman said as Nina unfurled herself from the undersized cruiser. Her tailored uniform fit perfectly, and her dark curly hair fell to her shoulders. "It's the local fuzz of color and her sidekick, Tonto." He made Tonto sound nauseating.

Pike came around the cruiser and leaned against the hood. Except for a hunting knife strapped to his belt, he had no weapon.

"What's this, Tonto?" Justman asked Pike as he elbowed Naize, "Upland's best don't allow *Redman to carry gun*?"

"Pike Tso," Pike said. "We met at the Hopi Trading Post a couple of days ago."

"Yeah, I remember. But at that time, I didn't know you were going to be her Tonto sidekick."

"What are you doing here, Thomas?" Nina asked again.

"Heard you talking to that pipsqueak Duke on the police radio—" Justman shrugged his shoulders "—so I came over."

"He's not a pipsqueak; and he's a better cop than you'll ever be."

"He wouldn't make a pimple on a good lawman's ass and you know it."

Nina ignored the cliché. She rubbed her nose, and tried not to let her disdain of Justman interfere with the business at hand. "Naize?" Nina turned to him for an explanation.

Naize shrugged. "We were both on Highway 89. I was monitoring the sheriff's frequency so didn't hear your call. Justman radioed me and asked me to follow him."

"Screw you, Nina . . . with all due respect," Justman said with a grimace that turned into a smile. "But we don't have to answer to you. Anyway the question should be why are you and Tonto here? I'd think you'd want Holly gone so you'd have Troy, the love of you life, all to yourself."

"What was between Troy and me is ancient history," she said more loudly than she'd wanted.

"That's enough," Pike said staring down Justman, "and don't call me Tonto again, *belagana*."

"I am Hualapai," Justman said in a tone that let everyone know he did not like being called a white man.

"Walk and dress like a duck doesn't really make you a duck," Pike said.

Justman turned to Naize. "What the hell is he talking about?"

Naize held his hands up. "I'm not getting in the middle of this, but you do look white, *amigo*."

"Screw both of you," Justman said.

"Okay, okay," Nina said, "enough bickering. I suppose that since you guys are here, you can help with the search party."

"But here's the thing," Justman said. "Since we're technically out of town limits, and given that I am here and have a grip on the situation, the sheriff's department will probably handle the whole thing. So, I guess *you* can help *us* with the search party."

"By sheriff's department, I suppose you mean you? And why would the Sheriff want a missing person's case when it hasn't even been established that she's missing?"

"Well, here's the thing," Justman said again, "we know how close you are to Troy—" he smiled broadly "—so we're not sure you're the right person for the job."

"Give me a damn break, will you?" Nina said.

Pike and Naize let them squabble as they walked around the site.

"Sure," Justman said. "Sure, but it looks to Naize and me like she fell off her horse, right over there—" he pointed toward Pike and an area of tall weeds "—so if she isn't missing, where the hell is she?"

"Sometimes you amaze me with your brilliance," Nina said. "That's what the search party's for, for Christ's sake, to see if Holly's out here somewhere, injured or incapacitated, or something—"

"There's some blood over here," Pike said, "not much but still it's blood. And some broken weeds and two sets of barefoot footprints. I'd say one was Troy's, but the other is much larger and more defined, like a big guy carrying a heavy load."

"Are you sure?" Nina asked. "Both were barefoot?"

"Sure I'm sure," Pike said, "and Holly didn't just fall off her horse. It looks like her horse was spooked and she was thrown. It's an old Indian trick. You jump out from behind a bush or tree, startle the horse, and it throws the rider."

"I hate horses," Justman said.

"An Indian who hates horses, huh?" Nina laughed at Justman, but she closely watched Pike. Even though he was a rookie, he was already showing the quality it would take to become a good cop. Troy must have seen something in him too, because he'd gone out of his way to persuade Pike into becoming a cop for Upland instead of the Navajo police department in Window Rock. "Pike will be a good addition to the department," Troy had said when Nina objected to being his nursemaid for a week. "He's not only tough but he also knows a thing or two about Indians and he'll have easy access to the reservations, something we've needed around here for a long time." Nina could see that now, she admitted to herself, and was a little relieved that he was with her. "So you think an Indian jumped from a bush, startled her horse, she fell, and then he what? He kidnapped her? Is that your theory?"

"I said it was an old Indian trick, not an Indian. But, on the other hand, there are also a couple of crossed feathers lying on top of splotches of blood. They could have been placed there on purpose."

"What kind of feathers?" Nina asked.

"Bird feathers," Justman said, chuckled, and jabbed at Naize who frowned.

Pike ignored him. "Eagle maybe or hawk, but they're not fresh. The quills are dried out, so they've been around for a while."

"Feathers, okay," Nina said. "I certainly don't want any run-ins with the Indians right now. I'll bow out and let these two deputies extraordinaire run the search party, but since we're here—" she shrugged and pulled a long-handled Mag Light from the cruiser and flashed it around the site. The sun had almost set and the floor of the forest had become murky black, but she could clearly see two sets of prints leading toward the river and broken weeds and branches were prevalent.

"So rookie, I see the blood spots that would indicate that Holly might have fallen, and a trail leading toward the river, but no indication of abduction. It looks like she fell, and then maybe wandered to the river. Troy then followed her trail later."

"Those are not a woman's tracks and certainly not boot tracks, which I assume she would have been wearing," Pike said.

"Tonto's right," Justman said. "Now that I think about it, I'd bet she was kidnapped, and by an Indian."

Nina shinned the light directly into Justman's face. "Be nice, asshole. Why the change of heart?"

"The feathers," Justman quickly said, "eagle or hawk feathers, lying on the ground, beside the blood. I didn't think much of it at first, but now I believe it's a symbol: the eagle, a native bird that the Apache revered, and the crossed feathers signify the Indian dominating the white man."

"Christ," Nina said, "that's all we need, Indians on the warpath."

"Warpath indeed," Naize said. "And this feather thing is all hooey anyway, to my knowledge, Indians—Apache or otherwise—never used feathers to show dominance. That's stupid. And, even if it were true, it would be common knowledge around here, and anyone could have left feathers, even the damn bird."

Nina flashed the light back at Justman.

"I'm sure I read that somewhere," Justman said, a little taken aback. "It's the only explanation."

"And with that, Kemosabe," Nina said to Pike, "you stay here with Justman and Naize. I'm going to see if I can find us some volunteers. I'll send them out to you asap."

"So now we're friends?" Pike said as she left, but she did not respond.

8

When Nina arrived at the saloon, Kid and Blondie were in the pool table room. Kid was showing his mother how his stroke had improved and how it was as good as anybody else's, if not better. J.C., the always-dependable Dana, and Hog were tending the saloon. Hog Stevens had just returned from a motorcycle ride and was actually drinking a beer instead of working. Though known as a biker, Hog was a mild-mannered giant, a full six feet, six inches tall, broad with a thick burly neck, a large round jovial face, and a stomach that gave him his name. He treated Dana with love and respect which endeared him to everyone at the saloon.

J.C. looked up from washing bar glasses and watched as Nina stood in the doorway between the pool table room and the bar so that both sides of the saloon could see and hear her.

"Listen up!" she said in a commanding voice. "I have an announcement to make."

J.C. was surprised when the room went quiet almost immediately, and everyone turned to look at her. He'd seen this crowd carry on through gun shots with barely a flinch.

"Holly rode her horse down by the river behind her house this afternoon and either fell or was thrown, and the horse came home without her," Nina continued.

Everyone knew who Holly was so there were some oohs, ahs, and no shit comments before the chatting clatter began again as they turned back to their more important lives.

"There's more," Nina yelled. "Troy wants to form a search party tonight, right now, to go out and look for her. He's at his house waiting for anyone who wants to join him there, and Officer Pike and a couple of sheriff's deputies will be coordinating the search down by the river if anyone wants to join them there."

Falling from a horse or getting lost in the forest were common enough occurrences around Upland that most patrons simply ignored Nina's request and turned right back to doing what they were doing.

"What the hell," J.C. hollered. "This is my brother's wife she's talking about here. So this bar is officially closed, now get your dead asses up and let's go find her."

"Most of these idiots will just go to another bar," Dana said. "I'll stay here and keep the bar open by myself. You and Hog go help Troy."

J.C. agreed and eight people including Blondie, Kid, Hog, and Nina followed him to Troy's house while a few that knew the river area well enough went directly there, and a couple on horseback took the most direct route through the forest.

At the house, Troy thanked them all for coming and briefed them on what had happened. "At first, I though she'd simply fallen off of Chance," he told them, "but it looked more like there had been a scuffle, and she's been kidnapped or something."

"That's crazy thinkin," Hog quickly said. "Who the hell would do such a thing?"

"I don't know, but—"

"She's simply fallen off like you said and she's out there somewhere," J.C. said."

"Maybe, but I found some blood."

"What the hell does that mean?" someone asked.

"I don't really know, maybe nothing."

"Well, there you go then," J.C. said. "Let's go find her."

Blondie stayed behind to look after Jesse while the rest formed a line eight abreast with Troy and Nina on the flanks so no one would get lost. They covered as much of the woods as possible on both sides of the trail Holly and Chance had taken. Some had flashlights, but the full moon provided ample light for the rest as they trampled through the forest for more than an hour until they reached the river.

Deputy Justman was nowhere to be found.

But Naize and Pike had stretched a road map—the only map they had with them—across the hood of Naize's truck and they directed the search by assigning groups to different areas they'd penciled in on the map. They gave each group orders to report back to them before going home for the night.

9

Sheriff's Deputy Thomas Justman had not hung around for the search but, without explanation or excuse, had left Deputy Naize in charge and headed straight for the Hopi reservation, and for good reason. He knew who had taken Holly and why, and could not believe his good fortune. It had produced an unbelievable opportunity of a lifetime for him. His mind raced as fast as his truck as he sped up the dark rutty reservation road, the truck bouncing almost uncontrollably.

Justman knew the area well. He had grown up outside of Tuba City on the border of the Hopi reservation. He had ridden the same school buses to the same schools as most of the Indian kids in the area. He never knew his real father, and his mother was white (white trash the Indian kids had called her) but his stepfather, Jay Uqualla, was Hualapai. When Justman's classmates assured him that he was a Casper and not Indian, he refused to listen. Whether he was in fact Indian or even had any actual Indian blood was of no consequence to him because his stepfather had raised him as Hualapai and had instilled in him a belief that he too was indeed a true Hualapai. And he believed it. Not only had Jay Uqualla taught him the ways of the Hualapai but when he died he left Justman a room full of tribal paraphernalia that he had collected over the years—drums, moccasins, bracelets, headgear—all authentic artifacts fashioned and used by tribal members for over a hundred years. They were priceless. But more importantly, they were the sort of objects Justman would need to participate in Indian ceremonies, which he did often. In the beginning, it was almost exclusively visits to the Hualapai at the Grand Canyon. But now, for convenience sake, it had become mostly nearby tribes, Apache, Hopi, or Navajo.

It was at a Hopi powwow that Justman had befriended the Indian who called himself Red Hawk, and whom Justman had thought to be confused and muddleheaded from a rough life or drug overuse or some other malady. At that time, sitting close to a bonfire and smoking something stronger than weed alone, the Indian had insisted that he was one of the few, if not the only, pureblood Indian left, that all other Indians were contaminated with white blood, and that he wanted to go to an abandoned Indian stronghold and start anew with some beautiful maiden. Disserted well over a hundred years ago by Apache Chief Cochise, the stronghold was well hidden deep in the forest on the side of Shadow Mountain. And, he had mentioned "the woman Holly" specifically. Justman of course had laughed and thought he was joking, but had told him that, though married and therefore not a true maiden, Holly was indeed beautiful and would make a good candidate, and that he too had eyed Holly on more than a few occasions.

Justman had no idea just how serious the Indian had been.

Red Hawk lived in one of a few dilapidated houses on the side of a steep hill on an area of the reservation that was only two dirt streets wide, one fifty feet above the other and both scratched into the mountainside by luckless miners long before the 1848 treaty of Guadalupe Hidalgo defined the reservation borders. Justman eased his truck to a stop directly in front of the Indian's house. He sat there for a moment and watched for movement. Next door, the curtain drew back then quickly closed, a dog barked from close by, but nothing stirred within the Indian's house. Justman didn't think the Indian would be dumb enough to bring Holly here before taking her to Shadow Mountain, but he wanted to be careful. He quietly slid from the truck, pulled on a pair of latex gloves and, with revolver in hand, slowly moved up the dirt path to the stoop. Then, without warning, he rushed through the front door, ready to fire if needed. He found neither the Indian nor Holly.

Justman wandered about the one-room structure for a few minutes considering his situation, his connection to Red Hawk, and his options. He'd seen the place before so there was no need to linger. He picked up one of the many books that were lying about. He figured the Indian had read them long before his mind had gone to mush. Meticulously, Justman cut a variety of words from the book, then, using a mixture of water and flour from a glass jar he'd found in the cupboard, he crudely pasted the words onto a sheet of paper. He had always believed that when dealt a bad hand he could throw it away and lose for sure or, with a little guts, he could win big with it, if he played the cards right.

Poker playing—an odd vice for an Indian, he'd told himself many times, but still, he had no control— was Justman's one and only vice, and the higher the stakes, the bigger the thrill for him. But the game had recently dealt him a very bad hand. He always figured he had the ability to beat anyone. Lady Luck had been his to ravish for years. However, when The Lady turned on him, like a vengeful cat, her bitter claws pierced deep and painful, and she wouldn't let go no matter what he did. No matter how well he played, no matter how good his cards were, like a one-eyed jack-of-spades, she had turned a blind eye to him. He was now into the loosing streak for big bucks, sixty thousand to be precise, and the casino didn't take debt. Not because they were saints— the whole lot of them were worse than any mobster in Vegas or any bureaucratic politician Justman knew. Both with their grubby hands in the till, one skimming off the top, and the other (calling themselves state and federal gaming commissioners) heavily taxing whatever was left. In their greedy quest for all of the money, they allowed, even enticed, gamblers to bet big and therefore lose big. Even to the point of extending loose credit, and then collecting the debt through government-sponsored employer wage garnishment. All legal, of course, but all underhanded. Insolvency and losing his job with the county was an abyss Justman had found himself teetering over.

So, like most heavy gamblers Justman knew, he'd turned to the local loan shark, Calum Silverwood, to cover his ass, and had agreed to pay the twenty percent (twelve-thousand-dollar) vigorish Silverwood had demanded. Justman had signed everything he owned, including Jay Uqualla's Indian artifacts, over to Silverwood as collateral.

Silverwood—a gangly Navajo "businessman" who detested any reference to loan sharking, Mafia, or underworld even though his business consisted of lending money and using various tax rates as his basis for interest—had figured that if the government could charge twenty to thirty percent, so could he. And he had a way of collecting his money that would make any government envious. Dressed in a white man's three-piece Armani, Silverman had gone to visit Justman at the sheriff's office, of all places, to let him know that the debt was due, and had informed him that if he didn't pay up in a timely manner there would be an estate sale of his possessions. Justman got the drift. He recalled the untimely and gruesome demise of a guy on the reservation who, it was rumored, owed Silverwood a lot less.

Justman's first thought was to off Silverwood himself. Just take him out into the woods and blow his pock-marked head off. He could make it look like an accident or suicide or self-defense or whatever. There would be no big investigation, no big inquiry, because Silverwood had his hooks in many of Justman's peers and bosses. However, Silverwood was just a link in the chain of his underworld league of gentlemen. Maybe even the weak link, but that didn't matter because Silverwood's bosses would not, not in a million years, let Justman's debt go unpaid and he knew it. He had also considered simply disappearing. He could gather all his belongings; vanish among the tribe of Hualapai at the bottom of the Grand Canyon, never to be found. He had even gone so far as to pack up everything he owned in preparation for his exodus, and was waiting for the last possible moment, waiting for some miraculous opportunity that he had overlooked to materialize.

Jay Uqualla had taught him early on that when you open your mind to possibilities, opportunities would spring up when you least expected them and, sure as hell, now that the Indian had taken Holly, that opportunity had sprang to life. An opportunity of a lifetime, Justman figured. It would be so easy, so utterly fool-proof, that it made him giddy. Justman could repay Silverwood, have money in his pocket, and become a hero at the same time. He smiled; Lady Luck had finally released her claws, and he was headed for another winning streak. He placed the Indian's now mutilated book on top of the stack where the police could easily find it. But he made sure everything else was left in place. No one would know he'd been there, not even Red Hawk.

"Beautiful," he said to himself as he left the Indian's house, snapping the latex gloves from his fingers. "Beautiful."

10

Dead tired, Patrolman Pike Tso pulled his 1962 Corvette beneath the canopy of the large cottonwood tree that stood in front of his cabin on the north side of Upland. With two rooms and a bath, the cabin was small, even cramped by most standards, but the thought of living in an apartment in town nauseated him. The rustic structure was cobbled together at the outer edge of two wooded acres he'd purchased on contract from a friend of a friend of Hog Stevens, who had used it to butcher deer during the hunting season. Like his Vette, the cabin was a work in progress but, for Pike, the imposing view of the mountains made it worthwhile.

Everyone who had checked in for the search party had reported back by midnight. All sectors had been covered with no success in finding Holly, or any discernable clue as to what had happened to her. There had been some talk from disgruntled groups about never finding her because she'd disappeared on her own since she wasn't happy with Upland, home life, Troy, etc. Others were saying how tree debris had snagged her at the bottom of the river; there was also some Navajo talk about witches because of the proximity of Indian burial grounds. It never ceased to amaze Pike how callous some people could be when they weren't directly affected by the circumstances.

He revved the engine of the Corvette, listened to the rumble of the strong and solid 360 horses, and when he shut it down the engine died instantly, a sign of excellent compression. He'd driven the yet-to-be restored Corvette (with the top down because he couldn't get it to work at the time) from Flagstaff to St. Louis and back in early spring, just to follow famed Route 66 simply because long ago he'd watched a couple of old *Route 66* episodes on television. In the show two young men named Tod and Buz drove their new '62 Corvette along that route saving countless people from a myriad of troubles along the way, and Pike could see himself in that role, a savior of damsels in distress.

Inside the cabin, he put a pot on the small wood stove to brew a cup of Navajo herbal tea. His mother's blend of just the right amount of sage, greenthread and bidens was believed to give balance and harmony to the body and spirit. At least that's what his mother believed, but Pike simply liked the natural mellowing effect, much more subtle than beer, wine, or marijuana but still just as effective, and he didn't get drowsy or drunk and never woke up with a hangover.

Behind the cabin, Pike had already built a makeshift sweat lodge from local tree branches, grass, and mud, in the tradition of the old ways of the Navajo— small and tight for rapid heating and steam retention. As modern as Pike liked to believe himself to be, he still needed to keep in touch with his Navajo roots. He stripped down to his underwear, and with hot tea in hand, padded barefoot to the lodge, closed the flap behind him and set fire to the wood chips beneath two thin, concave rocks in the middle of the lodge. The rocks would heat up quickly and produce an abundance of steam the instant water hit them.

Pike leaned back against the raw structure and began sipping the strong, bittersweet brew. The effect was pleasing and calming, and by the time he'd drained the last drop from the cup, steam filled the diminutive room and, with muscles and joints relaxing, the tension of the day quickly evaporated. Traditional Navajo tea and sweat lodges were used for ceremonies or rituals, but Pike used his for solitude and meditation to help focus on what was important to him. He closed his eyes and let his thoughts wander, not only to the disappearance of Holly, but to the beautiful Nina Miller.

He'd met Nina the day he joined the department. She was tall, thin—but not skinny—with long legs and alluring, piercing brown eyes that gave him the heebie-jeebies when she looked at him. She had a come-hither habit of rubbing her nose with her middle finger when she was worried, and he found that beguiling and sexy beyond words. It all turned him into a bumbling schoolboy when he was around her. But he'd also quickly picked up on the fact that she secretly had eyes for Troy, which surprised Pike—but apparently no one else—since Troy was married and showed no visible romantic interest in her.

And Pike could tell right away that she thought of him as nothing more than her underling, a rookie cop to be pushed around. None of that, however, deterred his unyielding belief that someday, somewhere there might be a chance for him.

With that, Pike fell into a deep sleep.

11

By morning the search party had scoured the forest along the river for miles in all directions and all but two men had bailed out and gone home.

The two men, both from the Hopi reservation and on horseback, had made it north up the river, well past the reservoir, and stopped where natural caves and crevasses littered the river banks along the water's edge. They had found nothing. At the shallows along the edge of the rapidly flowing river they rested, watered their horses, discussed the possibility of going farther but, tired, hungry, and discouraged, they decided to turn back for home.

Within one of the caves, Holly's head tossed from side to side and her body twitched. She was dreaming of her ex-boyfriend, rodeo star Tex Bowman. In the dream, she on her filly and Tex on his stallion, toweringly handsome in tight jeans and wide-brimmed hat, were riding the circuit. They were happy and carefree, racing around an arena, a grandstand full of cowboys and cowgirls cheering them on feverishly.

When she heard muffled voices, speaking words she could not understand, her eyes fluttered and her dream changed, now she was lying on a bed that moved and crawled like fat earthworms, the naked Indian standing over her, devouring worm after worm. Then his black and white streaked face smiled pleasantly at her, his enormous manhood hinging merely inches above her.

"Taaa . . . aaay," he said, his voice hollow, and he pressed down on her and began rubbing between her legs, gently touching her inner thighs. She was frightened but also aroused and for a brief second she wanted to spread her legs and let him do what he wanted.

When she heard more voices, still muffled but close, she wanted to cry out to them, but only frantic breaths came through flaring nostrils and she kicked at the Indian. But he was gone, replaced by a fire that produced long flickering shadows on rock walls. And she was wide awake, in a cave by herself. As her head cleared, as her heartbeat settled, she recalled being dragged into the cave feet first by the rakehellish Indian of her nightmare.

Drowsy and terribly confused, trying to make sense of what was happening, she remembered stories of Indian ghosts roaming the Granite and Absaroka mountains in Montana, and she had heard similar stories of Indian ghosts in the Mazatzal and Superstition Mountains in Arizona. Was this Indian a ghost? Was he invading her mind, and maybe her body, while she slept?

The sun had crept high and bright and now streamed into the cave, coming through countless gaps around the boulder that blocked the cave's exit. She could see the boulder's outline perfectly. Pushing herself to her feet, she hopped toward the light and placed her face against the rocks, listening for the voices that had awakened her. She yelled through the cracks, but the sound she made was weak and high-pitched, and no one answered. She could smell the river. The air was moist and fresh, a relief from the stuffy cave. She tried to peer outside but could only see blue sky. It reminded her of the big sky of Montana and, fleetingly, she thought of Tex again. She remembered many episodes of lying in the back of his pickup truck, watching the deep blue sky while he pleasured her to fulfillment, and wondered where he was and what—or who—he was doing now.

"Why are you thinking of Tex and sex instead of Troy and safety?" she chided herself. And wondered if it was possible that she cared for Tex more than she'd realized? Maybe more than she cared for Troy. Would she always regard Tex as her savior, the one who had delivered her from the long and lonely months of being alone while living with her parents?

"Tex," she mumbled in a harsh muffled whisper. "Where the hell are you?" But when there was no answer, she leaned against the rock wall and fought back tears. Before she'd met Tex, she'd often awakened in the middle of the night frightened, crying and lonely. Parents who did not really care for each other, or her for that matter, had raised her. She had a grandfather who loathed her, thought of her as the devil's child, born out of wedlock. She had often prayed for anyone to love her and take her from surroundings where no one cared for her.

Then she'd met Tex and even though she'd called him a "Montana redneck," she'd hooked up with him almost immediately. He'd offered her a way out and companionship at the same time. He was her champion, her savior. She'd been attracted to that cowboy the minute she first saw him, slim and graceful, sitting high in the saddle of his bronco. He was courteous and smooth, with a bright quick smile and a bulge in his pants.

It was just over two years ago that Tex had brought her to Upland from Butte. They had, like scores of other rodeo riders, come to town to participate in Upland's *World's Rowdiest Rodeo* annual event. They rode the rodeo circuit together for nearly two years, and he'd been the one who taught her how to ride a horse and a man.

But those nights before she'd met her cowboy could not possibly add up to the fear and loneliness she now felt. Right now, all she wanted was Tex to be her savior once again. She wanted him to ride in on his steed and take her away from the cave, away from the ghostly Indian, away from what he might have in store for her. She curled up close to the fire, closed her eyes, and again dreamed of her wonderful, carefree time on the rodeo circuit with Tex Bowman.

12

Sunlight was filtering through linen curtains by the time Troy finally found sleep. He had spent most of the night franticly searching for any clue that might lead him to Holly. He'd taken the more aggressive route up the river by himself, but the search party before him had trampled any clue that might have been there. When he finally made it home and crashed, the possibility that Holly had disappeared on her own haunted him like a devilish nightmare, to the point that sleep only came in snatches. He was well aware of her unhappiness, but hearing the innuendos and grumblings about her from people he didn't even know had made him more acutely aware of how unhappy she must have been.

He was awake before noon, took a quick shower, and dressed in a fresh uniform. He found Jesse on the porch happily playing in his baby swing, blissfully unaware that his world might be unraveling with each back and forth movement of the seat.

Sitting at Jesse's side, Blondie glanced up from the local newspaper. "We tried to be quiet when we got up."

"I really appreciate you watching him for me."

"Want some breakfast?"

"Thanks, but I'm going to call Nina before I leave and have everyone meet me at the saloon for lunch."

"Well, don't you worry about Jesse any. I'll take good care of him. You go on and find his mother."

"What does the paper say?"

"Says she may have fallen, ran away on her own, or was abducted."

"Not much help," Troy said. He picked Jesse up and gave him a big hug and a kiss. "I'll find mommy, big boy, that's a promise. In the meantime, you behave for Blondie."

At the corral, Troy let the horses out of their stalls and fed them. But Chance refused to eat. She knew something was still amiss. She hung her head low and neighed softly. "I'll find her, that's a promise," he repeated his pledge to the horse.

13

It was early morning and still dark when Nina had her third cup of coffee, which she drank with two poached eggs and a piece of gluten-free toast. Troy always liked her with a flat stomach and small round butt and now wasn't the time to blow her diet. Though she vowed she would do everything in her power to help find Holly, she would, by all means, remain diligent with her eating routine. Just in case. Then, again, if they did not find Holly, how long would Troy be in mourning? And would he again be attracted to her, or was she wasting her time even thinking of such a thing? Was she being desperate or practical? The latter, with a capital P, she hoped.

Who else was there? She detested most other men. They were ill-mannered, ill-informed, and ill-dressed cowboy wannabes, or overweight, overeducated, and overbearing; nothing that suited her.

And because of her standards, she was still living in the same depressing house in which she grew up. It was an igloo in the winter, a sauna in the summer, and a breeze box in between. Her parents had simply given it to her after they finally built their "mansion" on the hill outside of town. Her father, being one of only a handful of medical doctors in town, had done well for himself and his family. Giving her the old residence was a magnanimous gesture, but the house was an embarrassment, as she could barely survive on her salary, let alone do anything constructive to the old building.

But, as usual, she dressed in an impressive fresh, highly pressed uniform before she drove back to the station. She could at least present herself as if she were single and loving it.

At the station, she spent the morning working on finding Holly, the only incident Upland had had in some time. She went over the list of possible enemies of Troy or Holly, but none was considered desperate enough to have committed a kidnapping. By noon, she thought about calling Troy to see if he was awake and wanted to meet her for coffee, or even a beer. She picked up the phone, shouldered it then let it slide back into its cradle. Should she be thinking about him this soon? Was she being too obvious? If Justman could see it, surely everyone could. She gave it an "I don't give a shit what they think" shrug, and was about to pick the phone up again when it rang.

"Good morning," she answered with perhaps too much enthusiasm.

"Not very professional for a police station," Troy said.

"I just knew it was going to be you."

"Oh?"

"Well, you know . . . how are you this morning?"

"I'm okay, I guess. Why don't you meet me at the saloon for lunch and we can discuss where we go from here?"

"I'm on my way."

"And make sure Pike is awake. We need everyone in on this."

She felt suddenly deflated. It wasn't going to be a rendezvous with Troy at the saloon, but a meeting with everyone. "Will do," she said frowning and hung up the phone. What the hell was she thinking? Of course it was a meeting. She needed to start thinking more rationally and get on with her life.

Nina grabbed the receiver again to call Pike but then remembered that he still had no phone even though it was a town requirement for all officers, so she called him on her hand-held radio. He answered instantly.

"Do you sleep with that thing?" she asked.

"I always sleep with that thing," Pike answered and chuckled.

"I'm talking about the radio. I don't care about any other *things* you might be sleeping with."

"The radio, that's what I'm talking about. I always sleep with it," Pike said still chuckling. "Do you have your mind somewhere else?"

"Troy wants a meeting," Nina said matter-of-factly, "at the saloon and a-sap. Should I let you walk or do you need a ride?"

"No, I'm going to start taking my own car. Your driving scares the hell out of me."

"Suite yourself, Rookie."

14

By mid-morning, J.C. and Kid were at the pool table playing One Pocket. It was their way of dealing with life's day to day hindrances, though mentally, both were preoccupied with Holly's disappearance. They had left Troy on his own after searching the river south, all the way to the Verde Bridge and back and, finding nothing, had returned home relatively early.

After fumbling through an uninspiring rack of fifteen balls, Kid wobbled the last one into his designated pocket, collected two bucks from his father, and began re-racking for another game.

"Come on, son," J.C. said, "rack'em to my advantage this time, and if you're going to beat me like a drum at least have the damn decency to act like you're interested." J.C.'s game had improved substantially since he quit smoking and drinking. He'd taken on most road players who had wandered into town in the last year or so, by either happenstance or knowing of J.C.'s reputation and hungry to take him on. J.C. was, however, well ahead of them in both money and games. But he still had trouble with his own son. And he would proudly confess such a dilemma to anyone who would listen.

"Do you think it was really an Indian who took her?" Kid asked as he half-heartedly set the triangle of balls into position.

"There you go, son. You can't be thinking about other things when you're playing. To win consistently, you have to put all your concentration into the game."

"Yeah, so you've told me like a million times. But Holly missing is serious and shouldn't be ignored."

"I know, I know. I feel the pain too, and we're not ignoring it. But at this point there's not much we can do but stay out of the way."

"So what about the Indians?"

"Well, okay, there are a few old time Indians scattered about, I'm sure. But I'd bet my last Washington that they're all tame and docile now—"

"Officer Pike would say that's a racist statement."

"All I'm saying is that they've been loose in those hills for longer than I'd know about, and to my knowledge, as meager as that may be, no one around here has been found dead or missing at the hand of an Indian for more than a hundred years. And there'll be lots of them joining in the search for Holly, so most—like Officer Pike—are good people. But remember this, son: some of them still like to drink, and that's the way it is."

"And your point would be?"

"Well, if you think about it, since we can't really offer anything by way of finding Holly, the best place to be during an ordeal like this is right here selling booze. That's how the Last Chance got its name, you know, it's the last chance they'll have to supplement their provisions with a bottle or two before leaving town, you know, for their search or whatever."

Kid rolled his eyes. "Yeah, you've said that like a million times too. But I thought it was the old time gold miners' *last chance* before they left town."

"Well . . . sure, that too, but mark my words, the tribe will be in soon enough."

"Uh-huh," Kid muttered, "but you said that no one has died at the hands of an Indian for a hundred years. What about the guy who was killed at the casino last year over a poker game? They think he was murdered by an Indian."

"That would be on the reservation, and they think it was a robbery gone bad or something. I'm not even sure it had anything to do with Indians even though it was on the reservation, if memory serves me."

"Some of the Indian kids at school say he's a ghost who came back to kill the white man, and that's why they can't find him."

"Come on, son. Let's play pool . . . a ghost huh? No, I'd say it was just some sore gambler who lost his money and found an easy way to get it back, or one who couldn't pay his loan shark, a Vegas connection, maybe. Something like that."

"They're saying spirits or ghosts or something because they built the casino close to sacred grounds." Kid continued with his theory.

"Those are just Indian ghost stories, son. They've been telling those since before I was around. You'll get used to them."

"Maybe he's the one who took Holly."

J.C. gave Kid a sour look. "You got me there son. A ghost, that's surely something to consider."

"They're not just ghost stories. I read about it at school. There have been lots of people to disappear in the mountains and are never found, not even their bones or anything."

"You read that in school?"

"The school library."

"Shouldn't you be doing real homework at the library?"

"It was homework. My teacher said I should do a report on it, instead of playing pool all the time."

"Humph, I don't mind you doing reports and such and keeping up with school work, and current events even, but don't you go neglecting your game—" he picked up the cue ball "—this, son, is your future. If you can control this little ball, you can control your life, your world. Someday soon we'll go on the road and you'll beat them all."

"I won't neglect my game, Pop. I'm as good as ever."

"I know. The only games I win anymore are the ones you let me win."

"Just greasing the wheels, like you taught me," Kid said with a large smile.

"Am I the only mark you can find?"

"No one else around here will play me anymore."

"Humph," JC repeated. "Maybe you're greasing the wrong wheels. And since you're not going to be serious about playing, I have a saloon to run." He unscrewed his pool cue and placed it in its carrying case. "But first, I suppose you can bring your winnings and buy us a soda pop or something." He led the way into the saloon.

15

Troy parked his cruiser at the curb beside the saloon, behind Nina's cruiser, which was behind Pike's Corvette, all three in a no parking zone. Nina was waiting for him.

"Is he inside?" Troy asked pointing at the Vette.

"He is," Nina answered. "Since the town doesn't have a patrol car for him, he wants to start driving his own vehicle instead of riding shotgun with me. I think he's afraid of my driving."

"You scare the hell out of me," Troy said. "Let's go buy him a cup of coffee for lasting as long as he did."

"Please," Nina said, following Troy into the saloon. "A couple of days is all."

Pike was sitting at the bar having coffee with J.C., who was leaning on his elbows from the other side. Unlike Troy and Nina, Pike looked well rested.

J.C. set up two more cups of coffee.

"I ordered beer," Pike said. "But J.C. told me that I will 'by God' be on duty twenty-four seven until we find Holly, and brought me coffee."

"That's the life of a small town cop, always on duty," Nina responded. She poured an abundance of cream and sugar into her coffee, stirred for a second, and then sipped.

"I didn't argue," Pike said watching her perform her coffee ritual.

Troy was about to start the meeting and stopped when a vagabond Indian slid through the door by pushing it open with his shoulders. He walked tall, erect, and broad. He was dressed in stained and tattered denim jeans, shirt, and a denim jacket short enough to reveal a wide silver studded belt with a hefty souvenir rodeo buckle, and a doeskin pouch that hung hip high from the side of his belt. A sweat-ringed black felt hat, decorated with white feathers held in place by a turquoise and silver studded band, sat squarely on his thin ragged face. Two jet-black braids of hair, each tied at its end with dirty yellow twine drooped long beside each ear. He marched directly to the back of the room where the bar turned a corner and met the wall, ignored the stool and leaned on the bar, semi-hidden behind the popcorn machine.

"He comes in every few days," J.C. said. "But never uses the door handle for fear of contacting 'the white man's disease.'"

"White man's disease?" Nina questioned and smiled at Pike. "Sounds horrible, maybe we'd better be careful hanging around here." She leaned over and shoulder-bumped Troy.

"I'd be vigilant," Troy said, "there are more whites in here than anything else."

Pike simply raised his cup again and smiled at them.

"But he never gets staggering drunk, not Indian style anyway," J.C. said.

"Indian style?" Pike questioned.

"The dreaded red man's disease," J.C. spoke loud enough for everyone to hear, and they all laughed.

"Yeah, I get it." Pike also laughed.

Again the door opened. This time Sheriff's Deputy Justman walked in. He looked puzzled when he saw the Indian at the end of the bar. "Hey, any news?" he asked as he took a seat beside Pike.

"None," Pike said. But he was keeping an eye on the Indian who was now intently watching Justman. "You know him?"

I've seen him around the reservation," Justman said, "I'm surprised to see him in here. Has he said anything?"

"About what?" Pike asked.

Justman shrugged but said nothing.

J.C. handed the Indian his drink. "He don't talk much until he's had his Seagram's."

The Indian stared at the whiskey and then at J.C.

"It's your friend, Chief," J.C. told the Indian. "It's okay."

The Indian looked dubious, but then slowly picked up the drink, looked deep into the glass, looked at J.C., looked at Justman and, seemingly satisfied that it was okay gradually put the glass to his mouth.

"He's not really a chief, you know," Pike said as he set his empty coffee cup on the bar.

"Hey, don't get all political on me, he likes being called Chief."

"You can't go calling someone chief just because he's Indian, it's an insult," Pike said, then turned to the Indian. "What's your name, Chief?"

Again, everyone laughed.

The Indian's black eyes shifted between Pike and Justman. His nose lay bent to the left making his right eye appear a quarter of an inch out of symmetry. He said nothing.

"His calls himself Red Hawk," Justman offered to the others.

"He gives me the creeps," Nina said, "the way he stares at me."

"Yeah, he stares like that at every woman who walks in," J.C. said. "Come to think of it, he's especially fond of watching Holly."

"Everybody stares at Holly . . ." Justman trailed off and looked at Troy.

"To tell you the truth," J.C. said, "I don't know how my brother landed her."

"Okay, okay, let's get focused here." Troy held up his hands. "We need to talk about what our next course of action is going to be. It's starting to look more and more like she was abducted." Troy had a hard time saying she, as if it were someone other than Holly, one of the two people he loved more than life itself. But he knew he needed to distance himself, and stay mentally detached, if he intended to find her himself without falling apart. "I'd hoped that she'd simply fallen off her horse and crawled to some kind of shelter. But we had a lot of people out there searching, and nothing."

"We found no real indication of an actual abduction either," Nina said.

"Don't forget the white feathers," Justman quickly added.

"Feathers?" Troy questioned.

"Pike found a couple of feathers at the site," Nina said.

"What's feathers have to do with it," Troy asked.

"Justman believes that, if Holly was kidnapped, it was by an Indian," Nina answered.

"Why would an Indian do such a thing?" Pike asked.

"That's why we're here, Newbie," Nina spoke directly to Pike, "to try and figure this out."

"Money," Justman said. "It motivates a lot of people to do things they wouldn't otherwise do."

"We don't have a ransom note," Nina said, "so that kind of leaves kidnapping hanging. But how about revenge, Troy? Do you have any enemies, Indian or otherwise, that I don't know about? I went over a possible list earlier, nothing made sense though."

Troy shrugged. "Not that I'm aware of."

"How about jealousy?" Justman asked. He was looking at Nina with a lopsided grin.

"Screw you, *Thomas*," Nina said. "You're the one who's jealous. I've seen the way you look at me . . . and at Holly for that matter. How do we know you didn't have something to do with this?"

"A good man would do wonders for you," Justman said.

"You might jerk-off to my picture, asshole. But that's as close as you'll ever get to me."

"Well, you are . . . um . . . nice to look at . . ." This time Pike's voice trailed off.

"Be, careful, Rookie." Nina uttered each word independently.

Pike held his hand up defensively and grinned at Justman. "Just saying."

"All right, you guys," Troy said, starting to feel a little uncomfortable that Nina was sitting closer than necessary, "there's nothing going on between Nina and me, and I suppose that needed to be said, given our history. And there are some other inferences that need to be addressed also, just to clear the air, and so I suppose I'm the one who ought to bring that up too. I don't think it's any big secret that Holly hasn't been happy lately so there's been some talk about the possibility that she faked the fall and disappeared on her own—"

"That's ridiculous." J.C. stopped Troy. "If Holly wanted to bail on you, she would've told you to your miserable face, and then walked out."

"Never believed it for a minute," Troy said, "and never will. But since it's out there, I just wanted to make sure no one else was thinking it."

"Well, if anyone else is," J.C. now bellowed loud enough for everyone in the saloon to hear, "they can kiss my ancient ass and get the hell out of my bar while they're doing it."

"Take it easy, J.C.," someone said from the back of the room. "I say she fell off of her horse and she's just lost, and if you want to, we'll all go back to the river and start a new search right now."

"I'm okay." J.C. assured them. "It's just that that kind of shit pisses me off."

"We can tell." Nina grinned at Pike.

"Another search won't be necessary," Troy said.

"So where do we go from here?" Pike asked. "We have the feathers and little else."

"And the feathers don't mean anything, not really," Nina added.

"Anyone could have thrown them there," Pike said, agreeing with her.

"But don't forget they were perfectly placed." Justman reminded them. "So they must have had some importance to someone."

"Justman thinks the feathers indicate dominance of the Indian over the white man," Nina said.

As usual, the Indian that Justman had called Red Hawk stood beside his stool listening intently. He finished his drink, carefully set the empty glass on the bar, stared into it briefly and then, head hanging, sauntered toward door.

Again, everyone turned and looked at him.

"Look at his hat," Justman shouted. "Look at the band, there's a couple of white feathers missing."

Everyone stared. His hat had three white feathers where five used to be.

"Hold on." Troy held out his hand to stop the Indian. "Tell us about the hat."

Red Hawk turned, looked at Troy, then Pike, and then locked eyes with Justman. "The spirit, he took her," the Indian blurted. "Not me. I did not do it." With that, he bolted out the door.

"What the hell does that mean?" Troy hollered and tried to get up, but they were all sandwiched in their seats by the close proximity of the others. By the time they were up and through the door, the Indian had vanished into the park across the street. They scattered and searched to no avail.

On the way back to the saloon, Justman pointed out a folded paper stuck behind the windshield wiper of Troy's cruiser.

"Was this here earlier?" Troy asked Nina as he retrieved the paper and unfolded it.

"I'm sure we would have noticed it," Nina answered. "You would have noticed it for sure."

Troy unfolded the note, read it, then passed it to Nina.

I have her if you want to see her ALIVE put one thousand one hundred dollar bills in a canvas backpack and drop it over SQUAW BUTTE before noon tomorrow if I see any one else in the area she is DEAD

"I'm sorry," Nina said after reading the note and passing it on to Justman. "At least it gives us hope that she's still alive."

Justman hurriedly scanned it and handed it off to Pike. "But now we know who did it."

Everyone looked at him.

"That fucking Indian—" he pointed toward the park "—who else? He must have put the note on your car before he went into the saloon."

"You were the last one in." Nina reminded Justman.

"Meaning what?"

"You two quit bickering," Pike said." It isn't helping."

"Kidnapping, even when the ransom is paid, rarely turns out good," Troy said misty-eyed and led the way back into the saloon. "Now we have an even bigger decision to make. He must have her hidden someplace and if we go charging onto the reservation we might frighten him into doing something stupid. And if we call the tribal police, it could be the same thing. "

"Somebody needs to go search his place." Justman suggested.

"I can't believe he got away so easily," Nina said.

"Now who's the newbie?" Pike looked at Nina and grinned. "Once he was across the street, there was no way we were going to catch him."

"How would you know that?"

"He's an Indian." Pike shrugged his shoulders.

"Or, maybe he has an accomplice," Nina said, "who picked him up."

"No . . . no," Justman said. "He'd be working alone."

Pike reread the note. "Drop it over Squaw Butte, what does that mean?"

"From the airplane," Troy said. "Squaw Butte is a remote area in the wilderness high enough for anyone there to see three-hundred and sixty degrees for miles. If anybody goes up there, he'll know."

Pike whistled. "A hundred thousand, dropped from an airplane."

"The guy knows what he's doing," Troy continued. "The canvas backpack will hold together and it will be easy to carry."

"The Indian doesn't look that smart," Nina said.

"He's a lot smarter than he looks or acts," Justman told her. "He was raised by whites and likes to read . . . and he reads books, lots of books."

"Justman, you seem to know a lot about him," Troy said. "How about you going up to the reservation and checking out his house?"

"I can't do it," Justman answered. "But I'll call Naize if you want, and ask him to go."

"Not necessary." Pike spoke up. "If he's on the reservation, I'll go first thing in the morning when he least expects it and bring him in for you."

"Is that the best we can do?" Troy asked. "A rookie?"

"I believe that's why you hired me," Pike answered, "to cover the reservation."

"I'll go with you." Nina told Pike like it was an order.

"No," Pike said. "I agree with Troy, we don't want to show up in force. I think I'll have a better chance by myself, driving my car instead of a police vehicle."

"She should go," Troy said. "Backup wouldn't hurt and she has a weapon. But wear civvies, and Pike's car is a good idea."

"I agree." Justman made sure he was heard. "And if he's not there, make sure you search his house thoroughly."

"Okay, that's settled," Troy said before Pike could object. "But be careful and keep in constant contact at all times. In the meantime, I'll go get the money together in case I have to make the drop."

16

Red Hawk ran with the speed and agility of a warrior from a long gone past. He ran well into the night, all the way back to the reservation, up the hill, and into the building he had called his place for well over a year. He wasn't running from the police any longer, they had given up their pursuit quickly. He was running because he liked to run. He could run for hours, covering miles without tiring. It was simply the fastest way from one point to another.

Red Hawk was born in a Flagstaff medical center to a fourteen-year-old petite Indian girl impregnated by her uncle. Overseen by a white government agent, an all-white staff delivered him. Though premature, he was exceptionally large and his mother died giving birth. The medical center never bothered to record a tribe or reservation affiliation.

A white couple, seeking to alleviate themselves of the socially imposed remorse they felt for what the white man had done to the red man hundreds of years earlier—though they themselves had absolutely nothing to do with it—immediately adopted him. He was never gazed upon by his real mother or father, never given a native name, and never blessed by any shaman of any tribe. His white parents, who understood neither Indians nor their traditions of manhood, gave him a white name and as he grew, he longed for a name more fitting to him and the ways of his people. He often wondered what his Indian name might have been had he been raised by his real parents, both of whom were Navajo he was sure, not Kaibab nor Hopi nor Hualapai nor Apache, but pureblood Navajo, which made him the same. And he wanted an Indian name, big and bold and fearsome like Crazy Horse or Running Bear or Soaring Eagle. He did not want to be a Thomas or a Billy or a Mark or anything White. He real parents would have named him Red for the color of his skin and Hawk for his hawkish facial features, so that was what he decided to call himself.

Almost from the moment he opened his dull brown eyes to gaze into the dazzling turquoise eyes of his adoptive mother and deep blue eyes of his adoptive father, he knew he did not belong in their world. And as a full-sized teen, he could see and feel the disparity between him and the whites as he wandered the streets of Flagstaff. He walked tall and proud, had dark, reddish skin, high cheekbones, a prominent beak nose, and straight jet-black, shoulder-length hair that often swirled in the wind, traits anyone should be proud of. And though white people would nod at him and say "hey" in Indian fashion and were friendly enough, he could hear them whisper as he passed, "Why are those *Indians* allowed off the reservation? They are so ugly."

White people no longer feared Indians, Red Hawk often thought, and wondered how this could have happened to such a righteous and ferocious people.

Somehow Indians had become passive, tame, insignificant, repugnant, someone to be adopted out to relieve a white person from the horrors of a two hundred-year-old guilt complex. To Red Hawk, all Native Americans now belonged to an underclass of utterly disadvantaged people, displaced and downtrodden by the white man, and this gave him the right, no, the obligation, to reject the white establishment in which he was raised.

He was sure that if the great Navajo Chief Manuelito or Hoskininni or Chee, or even the Apache Chief Cochise or Geronimo, or any of their true-blood descendents were here now, those white eyes would look the other way in fright, and run in panic. Red Hawk wished he could create such panic in the eyes of the whites. As a young man he had often tried and, as a result, had learned to fight by calling upon and believing that the spirits of those great warriors of the past were at his side. He believed they were there to guard him, to protect him, to help him through the difficult fights he encountered. He could see them and feel them deep in his soul as he fought fiercely, sometimes without control or consideration; he attacked, spit and bit, pinched and kicked, punched and hammered, more often than not taking the beating himself, and always—always—swearing revenge when he succumbed. He would wait days or weeks and waylay his foe without thought of consequences, and usually came out on top of his sneak attacks, though his nose had been broken twice and now lay slightly canted to the left of his face. A deep-seated hatred for the white man manifested itself in him as he grew and as he craved and sought his true destiny.

He especially hated the white policeman Justman, who pretended to be Indian, and who would always believe that he had taken the woman Holly. But he had not, not really. He would probably kill Justman given the chance. Find a knife and stab him through the neck, maybe. And he now feared and loathed the white policeman Troy, the white husband of the woman Holly. Maybe he would kill the policeman Troy too, maybe.

Red Hawk had first seen the woman Holly at the river on her horse and, after that he had watched her many times in the saloon. And he had even seen her on the streets by the park as she strolled alone on warm summer days. She had smiled at him twice. No woman had ever smiled at him as she did. She was dark complected with large brown eyes that sparkled when she smiled at him and long black hair that also swirled when the wind blew. She was Indian like him, not white. She was pureblood like him, not contaminated. She was perfect.

In the not too distant past, Red Hawk had attended numerous Native American powwows and meetings—real Indians, he'd heard, with real Indian names. But what he found was dancing, barbeques, drinking, and parties; what he found were Apache, Navajo, Hopi, and Yavapai assimilated into the white man's culture with lots of Lukes and Larrys and Thomases and Carls and Marks; what he found was whiskey, marijuana, peyote, and other drugs that set his mind free; what he found were red-brown, pseudo-Indians who saw *him* as the outcast, a throwback from old times they said, not a modern Indian as they were. A black cloud, filled with the ghosts of their ancestors, hung over him and tormented him with archaic beliefs, they said. And indeed he yearned to be a part of the old ways of his ancestors, and dreamed for a new beginning for all Indians, untainted by others, as pure as springtime mountain streams—as pure as the woman Holly.

Though Red Hawk had been a poor student in the white man's school, he had, with pride and enthusiasm, studied books of great warriors of the past, and was now sure he knew how the Indians of today had become so watered down, so utterly devalued in stature and gumption. In the mid 1500s, the Spanish explorer Coronado led an expedition of white men across the Rio Grande from Mexico, looking for the rich city of Cibola, a city built of gold. In the beginning, the friendly native men helped Coronado in his quest. Simultaneously, however, Coronado's men helped themselves to the women of the tribes, betraying the very men who supported them, and thus began the dilution of the bloodline. Seeking revenge for the betrayal, the natives banned together and furiously drove the Spaniards back to where they'd come from. When the explorers returned home, they talked of the natives and referred to them as Apache—enemy of the white man—who promised punishment and death to any white man infringing upon the domain of their ancestors.

Then, in the 1800s, Peralta, a prospector and his army of men from Mexico, came looking for the fabled city of gold. Unlike Coronado, Peralta's men treated the Indians as brothers giving them gifts of colorful clothing, blankets, trinkets, and mules to eat. Over the next decade, the Mexicans hauled a million dollars worth of gold concentrate across the border. However, like Coronado's men, they also began impregnating the woman, mostly young girls. This didn't particularly bother the elders of the tribes who were content with the bribes of warm blankets and mule meat. But the youthful, aggressive tribesmen became restless and jealous. As more and more of the young woman weakened the native bloodline by giving birth to the white men's babies, the tribesman, provoked by the brave warriors of the tribes, reached their limits. They pressed Cochise, chief of his band of Apache, to join forces with Coloradas and mount a surprise attack on the Mexicans, stripping them of their gold findings, and annihilating the ones that did not make it back across the Rio Grande.

Red Hawk idolized Cochise and the warriors for their stand against the "white eyes" to the point of memorizing Cochise's family lineage: Cochise married Dos-teh-seh, daughter of Coloradas, and had two sons, Taza and Naiche. And Red Hawk believed Ta-ay, younger sister of Dos-teh-seh, was to marry Hoskininni, the great warrior of the Navajo.

Not only did Red Hawk study the books, he astutely listened to the teachings of those few Navajos skilled as shamans or *yataalii* or witches who could perform the rituals and would tell him the way. He absorbed their knowledge, believed in the calling, and thought—without doubt, fear, or reservations—that he too had the gift, and he heard the spirits in the winds, rustling the limbs and leaves in the tall trees, confirming his beliefs. He memorized, in minute detail, what was necessary to do the calling. He understood that the only purebloods left (besides himself and the woman Holly) were those who lived in the shadows of the mountains, not the docile ones on the reservations, but the ones who lived in the wilderness, the ones that most feared but no one spoke of, the ones that only those blessed with the power of the Witchery would admit existed. But he knew. He knew they were there. And he longed to join them for a new beginning of pure Indians.

It was at the Navajo powwows and midnight meeting of the Towering Cliff Clan of the Rock Gap People in the remote forest hills of the Navajo reservation that Red Hawk began his quest of calling to the spirits in earnest. He had called Hoskininni forth and had spoken to him and told them of the woman Holly, how she had dark skin with a reddish glow, coal black hair, and large bright brown eyes. She was a beautiful Indian maiden, the one for whom Red Hawk's heart beat; she was perfect for him and his new beginning. He ached for a female companion to share in his dream, had always yearned for such companionship, but all had rejected him, until now. Now he had found a means through the calling of the visitant spirit.

17

Late in the evening Holly awoke alone. There were no dreams and no Indian, only the faint odor of masculinity. It was not at all unpleasant. It reminded her of Tex.

There would be no Tex though, or Troy either. She was alone, without help or guidance. She could lie there and hope or dream or cry, but none of that would help. No, now was the time for her to step up, compose herself, and think clearly. She must think of survival. Forget Tex and the Indian, and Troy, for the moment at least. She had to figure some way to endure, some way out. "What would a survivalist do?" she asked herself. "What would Tex do? No, that's not the right question. What would Troy do?" But, in her mind, that didn't fit quite right either. "No, what would a *female* do? A female survivalist, maybe, what would she do?"

Celie in *The Color Purple* was a survivalist, but then all of Alice Walker's characters were survivalists. Scarlett O'Hara in *Gone with the Wind* was a Margaret Mitchell survivalist. But that kind of surviving was really just figuring out life and living with what it gave you. This was a different kind of surviving. This was staying alive, and that was what she wanted to do. Of all the books she had read, surely there was one about a girl escaping from the evil around her and then surviving in the wilderness. There had to be hundreds, she thought. But she could not recall one in which some female character, even a minor one, did that.

"Think, girl, think," she told herself. "There has to be a way." She was a descendant of a family from Mexico that helped settle Butte, a family that staked gold claims in the Montana mountains. And on her mother's side, her great-grandmother was a Navajo who had been with a band of renegades that wandered north to join the Crow and Chief Plenty Coup in their great battles against Red Cloud and Crazy Horse and the Lakota. She hadn't considered her Indian heritage in years. Not until the paint-faced freak reminded her. But now, she reasoned, it would be that Indian lineage that would not allow her to lie here, in this cramped cave, and simply die, or do the bidding of some crazy-ass from the past, ghost or not. Telling herself that, however, and doing something about it were two different things entirely, but she knew she would not allow herself the luxury of giving up so pitifully.

She thought about the bindings that held her numb and lifeless arms behind her. The bindings were around her wrist which allowed her arms to move somewhat. "What if—" she asked herself and she rolled up on her knees and shoved her hands below her rear, performing the act of setting herself free as she thought about it. She pushed hard, the cords dug into her wrists but stretched, and then her hands squeezed past her hips. She fell backwards, closed her eyes and held her breath to endure the pain as, one leg at a time, she forced her boots between her bruised and bleeding arms until her arms were finally in front of her. She lay still for a moment catching her breath, then, using her teeth, she slowly and painstakingly gnawed at the knot that bound her wrists until her hands pulled loose. A few more minutes of rest to allow the numbness to abate, then she simply reached down and untied her ankles. "There," she told herself, "that's thinking like someone who wants to survive." She could feel the freedom.

Free of her bindings, she staggered to the front of the cave and, with all the energy she could muster, she shoved at the boulder that blocked the entrance. Her boots dug into the dirt slipping and sliding for traction. She'd seen the Indian move it with ease, but for her, it would not budge. "God," she cried, "please." She'd come so far, endured so much, just to fail. The idea of enduring another night in the cave, and the possibility of encountering the Indian again terrified her.

Hysterically, she pulled at some small rocks that filled the gaps around the boulder. Small shafts of moonlight and clean air filtered into the cave as the rocks dislodged, but the gaps were not big enough for her to squeeze through. With bare hands, she began digging at the dirt around the bottom of the boulder. She dug until she was exhausted but made little headway.

Energy spent, she collapsed back onto the comfort of her dirt bed. Her back ached and her legs were frighteningly numb. She could see fresh blood oozing past the slit in her trousers. She leaned her back against the jagged rock wall facing the now dimming firelight and, trying so desperately not to, she began to cry until she once again slept.

18

Both Pike and Nina dressed in Levis, plain shirts, and Levi jackets, typical local attire, in an attempt to blend in, as much as they could driving a Corvette on Indian land.

They arrived at the administration building on the Hopi reservation early in the morning, introduced themselves, and asked for information on an Indian calling himself Red Hawk.

Mark Palmer a.k.a. Red Hawk, they found out, was born in a Flagstaff medical center. His Navajo mother died giving birth and a white couple, Dan and Julia Palmer, raised him. Because he was Navajo, he had no legal status on the Hopi reservation or any rights to housing, though, as a Native American, he was welcomed at hall meetings, powwows, or any other social gatherings. And though his mental capacity was suspect, he was not hindered from taking refuge on Hopi land. According to reservation scuttlebutt, he was indeed living in an abandoned mining camp in the hills at the north edge of the reservation. Hopi tribal laws also protected Palmer, which meant that Pike could investigate but could only make a civil arrest and then only if he was in uniform. He would also have to process Palmer though the tribal police department before removing him from the reservation. Pike and Nina changed into their uniforms so they could visit Palmer without a tribal police escort.

The only road, rugged and rutted, leading up to the camp, and Palmer's house seemed impossibility steep. The Corvette stayed in low gear, engine revving past four grand, as it pulled ever so slowly upward. Abandoned rusty relics of pickup trucks and cars proved that two-wheel drive vehicles had been pulling the hill for years so Pike pushed forward.

The old buildings, condemned years ago by tribal elders, were long past their usefulness and now used only as flophouses by druggies, alcoholics, and otherwise homeless, transient Indians of various tribes. The buildings looked dangerously ill-conceived with their fronts at street level and their backs overhanging the slope of the hill, and all supported by pillars of tall, slender, and ancient timbers.

The road turned left and flattened out in front of the first row of houses at Pike's left. He drove slowly past the six dilapidated buildings. All appeared uninhibited, though he knew appearances could be deceptive. The narrow lower road turned right at the end of the shanties, ascended up another steep grade to the top road where a right turn put another row of decrepit buildings on Pike's right side overlooking the rooftops of the structures below. A dog, chained to a supporting pillar of the second house, barked and Pike could see a dust-covered curtain pull sideways, then close. After parking, he and Nina walked up to the door of that house.

Pike knocked. "We're looking for a friend of mine," Pike said, "and I'm not sure which house he lives in." Again the curtain moved slightly. "*Ya-tah.*" It was an old woman's voice, deep and raspy, speaking Navajo. She could have been sixty or a hundred.

"*Ya-tah-hey,*" Pike answered. "Do you speak English?"

"Somewhat well," she said and coughed.

"I'm looking for Mark Palmer. Do you know him?"

"Nah."

"How about Red Hawk?"

"Red Hawk, he evil."

"How is he evil?"

"He chant to do witchery."

"Maybe he's a shaman."

"No shaman, a witch, pure evil."

"Do you know where he lives?"

"You not tribal police. Why you want him?"

"We need to ask him some questions, that's all?"

"About witchery?"

"Sure, why not?" Nina said looking at Pike. She smiled and shrugged.

The old woman coughed, long and hard then caught her breath. "He next door, but he not home. He leave an hour ago, maybe. He chant to do witchery. I tell him he must do it where the spirit live. He go there sometime, maybe."

Pike knew she would be talking about some sacred burial grounds, but there were a lot of those in Arizona. "Do you know exactly where?"

"Zuni cause he crazy. He try witchery with the ancient Zuni, not the Navajo. He make big trouble if he do good."

"Zuni?"

"White man call it Zuni Well. But it not the right name."

"Do you know what she's talking about?" Nina asked Pike, whispering.

Pike nodded. "What's the right name?" He knew generally where Zuni Wells was, though he'd never been there. It was actually a small, shallow lake next to a large, very old Zuni burial ground. Stories abounded about hauntings and other strange things happening there, at the base of Shadow Mountain. But Zuni Wells was northwest of Upland and miles north of where Holly had disappeared.

"Lake of Many Spirit," the old woman answered.

Pike smiled. "Makes sense."

"Home of many spirit, I say, is best place for witch and witchcraft and skinwalker," the old woman said in a serious tone. "He go there for Witchery Way. He cause big trouble."

Nina frowned.

Pike smiled again. "Many splinter clans of the Navajo still believe in witchcraft and skinwalkers and such," he told Nina. But he wasn't aware of any Hopi true believers. "You are Navajo, enit?" he asked the old woman.

"Walks Around Clan, off the Big Reservation."

"Why are you here?"

"Walk'n around." The old woman suffered a coughing chuckle.

Pike laughed at her attempt at humor. "Okay. That's a good one." He nudged Nina and they headed next door.

"He not there," the old woman called after him, "you can go inside to see."

Pike waved at her. They left the Vette where it was, and crept down the steep grade between the buildings then ducked among the pillars that held up Palmer's house. They listened for movement or sounds. All seemed quiet, so they moved around looking for a trap door, hidden cellar, or box, anything that might hide a human, dead or alive. There was nothing but tall weeds, overgrowth, and years of trash. Slowly, they crept back up the hill, around the corner to the front of the house.

On the front stoop, Pike peered through the glassless window and saw no one. The door had no lock and probably never did. He stepped inside and again listened for sounds. Nothing.

"You can't do that without a search warrant," Nina said and followed him in.

"Hello, anyone here?"

No one answered.

The single-room building was surprisingly clean: the wooden floor, mopped and dust free; a mattress lay on the floor in the corner, neatly made with sheets and pillows with cases; an old but sturdy couch and coffee table sat on the opposite side of the room. A bucket of water sat beside a small kitchen sink at the back of the room. There were clean dishes on a drain board at one side, a toothbrush, toothpaste, and bar soap at the other side.

"Crazy but clean," Pike said.

"Don't make sense. He seemed like such a slime ball." Again Nina looked for chests, boxes, refrigerators, or closets where a person, dead or alive, could be hidden.

Wooden crates, stacked beside the couch and mattress, were piled with a variety of well-worn books. Candles sat on the edge of some crates, obviously used for lighting since the building never had electricity. Pike scanned over the books amassed by the bed. Six were set aside; he glanced over the titles of the first three:

Indeh: An Apache Odyssey
Navajo: A History and Culture
Western Navajo

The fourth, *The New Navajo: Taking Back our Pride and Power,* was heavily dog-eared. Pike thumbed through it. The bookmarked passages gave instructions on how it was up to the individual Navajo to preserve the Navajo blood line, suggesting that two purebloods should sequester themselves in a remote land and start anew. Pike laid the book aside. He liked being a modern American Navajo and wondered why anyone would want to return to the old ways. He examined another heavily dog-eared book, *The Witchery Way: Skin Walkers, Shape Changers, and Other Navajo Witchery.* A Navajo author and shaman named Sam Alton wrote the book. Pike had heard of Alton, who, at age 82, died some years back. Some had considered him a charlatan, but others claimed him to be a master. Pike had no idea he'd written such a book.

The sixth book, *Once They Moved like the Wind: Cochise, Geronimo, and the Indian Wars,* lay at the end of the stack by itself. When Pike opened it, he found pages riddled with holes. Whole words had been surgically removed. Pike recognized the typeface.

Beside the bed and almost hidden from sight, he found the only picture in the house, a single shot of Holly pinned to the wall. It was a publicity photo from when she won the Upland Rodeo Queen Pageant a couple of years back. She wore a white cowgirl outfit that made her look thin and dark complexioned, a remarkable likeness of a Native American, something Pike had failed to notice before, but something Mark Palmer obviously had not missed. Pike had met Holly only once since joining the department, and thought her extremely good-looking, but he hadn't given it or her much thought beyond that. Troy, though, had made it a point to tell him that Holly was a descendant of some tribe or another from Montana. But that was a claim made by many people these days.

"I think Justman is right about him being the one," Pike said.

"How's that?" Nina called from the kitchen area.

Pike pointed to four books stacked at his elbow. They're all about Apache and Navajo chiefs and warriors—"

"No law against that."

"He's obsessed with the old ways, and Navajo spirits and witchery and—"

"Indian mumbo jumbo doesn't make him our man."

"I know, but he also has a picture of Holly tacked to his wall beside his bed."

"So he's a pervert . . . any pictures of me?"

"He only likes Indians," Pike said and smiled. "But I have a shot of you beside my bed, if that makes you feel better."

"A little, maybe, but I don't want to hear about what you do with it."

Pike smiled again. "Probably wouldn't be all that exciting anyway. But there's more, one of the books has pages riddled with holes where whole words were cut from them." Pike handed the book to her.

Nina flipped the pages, whistled, and rubbed her nose. "Son of a bitch, I suppose it could be the same print as the ransom note."

"Come on, you know it's the same—"

Before they left, Pike examined the fire residue in front of the window that he'd noticed when he came in. It had been a small fire ringed with small stones sitting on a sheet of tin. Around the still-warm stones were telltale remains of smoking paraphernalia. Palmer had said he liked to smoke marijuana and peyote. Maybe he was doing opium or some other hard drugs as well. But why the fire, was he really trying to perform a Witchery Way?

Palmer had also said that an Indian spirit had taken Holly. Had Palmer been hallucinating when he abducted her, having sort of an out-of-body experience, seeing what he was doing but so high, so out of it, that he did not realize that he was the one doing it? Or, was he cleaver enough to try to cover up his own actions, knowing full well what he had done and was doing, thinking he could blame it on some supernatural force? If so, why the ransom note? Of all the things that Palmer might be, he was not materialistic. A hundred thousand dollars wouldn't mean crap to him.

With Nina following, Pike walked next door and knocked on the old woman's door again.

"I said to you, he no home." She hacked out the words and pulled the curtains only an inch back.

"You said he was trying a Witchery Way. Was he doing it in his house?"

"Many week ago. I told him house no good. Go to the spirits, I say to him."

"Did you show him how to do the conjuring or any calling?"

"He tried to use cow bone. But he must use the ancient bone of people, I say to him. And coyote bone too maybe. No cow."

"So you showed him how?"

"I laugh and show him, but maybe he too good now. Big trouble if he do good. Big trouble." This time her cough became disruptive. She let the curtains close and dismissed them that easily.

19

Morning sunshine warmed the streets of Upland, and a light breeze rustled the trees as the newly reestablished Forkner family, including baby Jesse in his carriage, strolled around town shopping and eating forbidden desserts. Kid proudly introduced his mother to anyone interested. "Hi, this is my mom." "Hi, this is my mom," he would enthusiastically say to friends and shop owners he knew. There was never a mention as to why she'd been absent for the past two years, only joy that she was here now.

Though their hearts still weighed heavy with the disappearance of Holly, the fact was, it had forced them to be together almost constantly as they watched Jesse for Troy.

"This is life, son," J.C. said to Kid. "It's a shame I didn't find it years ago."

"You had it, you just didn't know it," Blondie said.

"My blunder." J.C. admitted.

After an excellent morning, Jesse began to fuss so they returned to Troy's house where J.C. fixed burgers and drinks for all. Overlooking Holly's riding arena, watching Chance prance from fence to fence yearning for the return of her master, they continued to take pleasure in each other's company as a family while having lunch.

As the afternoon stretched into evening, J.C. and Kid left Blondie to tend to the baby and went to their apartment above the saloon for a shower and a much needed change of clothes. An hour later, Kid was done and out the door to "bang some balls around on the pool table," while J.C. primped.

J.C. took his time and when he came down the stairs with a spring in his step and humming Andy Williams' *Love Story*, he was clean shaven, dressed in crisp clean slacks and sports shirt, and feeling giddy at the turn of events in his life. Once again a family man with means, he had a son who was a world beater pool player, a wife who had come back to him, and a saloon that would support them in style. With that thought, his humming broke into song.

> *"Where do I begin*
> *"To tell the story*
> *"Of how great a love can be*
> *"The sweet love story*
> *"That is older than the sea*
> *"That sings the truth about the love she brings to*
> me . . ."*

Then, a sudden crushing feeling of rebuff and regret slammed him back to reality as he walked into the saloon. Kid sat at the far end of the bar with a familiar-looking guy who was drinking beer, joking, laughing, and slapping Kid on the back as if they'd been friends all their lives. Some old timers also sat at the bar partaking from the guy's pitcher of draft beer. He had long dark hair pulled back into a single ponytail, full unkept facial hair, was sloppily dressed, and yet handsomely baby-faced.

The joking and laughter stopped as J.C. approached. "Rabbit," J.C. said and straddled the stool next to him.

"J.C.," Rabbit answered, smiled and tipped his glass in salute of recognition.

"Dad," Kid said. "Rabbit was telling us about the funny things I used to do when I was a kid in California."

"That so?" J.C. asked without taking his eyes off of the long haired, wife-stealing, hippie. "I see you've added an earring to the mess."

"Three grand," Rabbit said and turned his head for all to see. "One carat diamond and fourteen karat gold stud; like it?"

"Makes you look like a pussy," J.C. said. "What are you doing here?"

"What the fuck do you think I'm doing, numb nuts?" Rabbit answered. "I come to get my woman back."

"She ain't your woman!" Kid said loudly and quickly jumped away from Rabbit. "She's my mother." He turned and headed for the pool table room.

"Sorry, kid," Rabbit said. "But your old man can't take care of her no more."

All but one of the old timers eased from their stools, and sauntered away, free drinks in hand. The house painter known as "Jiffy" stayed put. He grinned broadly. "Hey J.C., I guess you do know how it feels to have someone else screwing you wife," he said and snickered.

"You're one disgusting piece of shit, Jiffy," J.C. said. "Nobody wants to hear from you."

"Takes one to know one," Jiffy responded.

"I want to hear from him," Rabbit said. "Let's have the whole story, house painter."

"He screwed my wife," Jiffy explained, "and left me with his bastard kid to raise."

"No shit?" Rabbit said and laughed. "No fucking shit. Where's the kid now?"

"She lives with her mother in the house that I built while I live in a shanty at the edge of town," Jiffy said.

"Not exactly the truth as I remember it," J.C. said. "She's your kid that you couldn't take care of, and your wife ran you off because you're crazy as a loon, and since this is going to be a private conversation between the pussy and me, get lost."

"Fuck you," Jiffy answered. "This is a public establishment and I have a right to set here and drink my beer and laugh if I want, and I want."

"You know Blondie and I are still married—" J.C. turned to Rabbit trying to ignore an old nemesis to confront a new one "—and she came back to me as soon as she saw you for the low-life you are."

"She only come here because we were out of money, lamebrain," Rabbit said. "'cause I had a string of bad luck, and you know it."

"Bad luck my ass," J.C. said. "Like Jiffy here, you never could play for shit and you're too dimwitted to realize it . . . also like Jiffy."

"Screw you," Jiffy hollered.

"You only wish you could screw me," J.C. answered, "like I did your wife, maybe."

Red faced, Jiffy was in J.C.'s face in an instant. "Fuck you," he screamed, spittle flying.

"Is that the best you got? You're right back where you started. So am I supposed to say, you only wish you could fuck me?"

"Fu . . . fu…" Jiffy couldn't bring himself to say it again and couldn't think of anything else. He sat down, took a sip of his beer, and brooded.

"Like you're any better at playing," Rabbit said to J.C. but laughed at Jiffy's cowering. "You probably couldn't run three fucking balls in a row, you washed up old fool. Do you really think she came back for you, you crazy old bastard. What are you, like twenty years older than her? You got nothing to offer her but gray hair and a shriveled peter."

"Maybe I do, and maybe I don't," J.C. said. "But the fact of the matter is she's here."

"She come back to get her son, dumbass," Rabbit said, "not be with you. And now that I'm flush again, she'll be ready to hit the road with me again after I talk to her. And we'll probably take the kid too."

"Maybe she will and maybe she won't, but if she is ready, it won't be with you. And there's no way you'll take the boy. I'll damn sure see to that."

"Look who's dimwitted now, you old fool. You couldn't stop me from seeing her if you wanted to. I think you're just damned scared they'll go with me, and leave you here in this shithole to die all by yourself."

"I'll admit she hasn't committed to staying yet. Not for me or the boy. But as far as stopping you, you should know that my brother is the law in town and I can have you arrested for vagrancy or something I'm sure, and then I'll have him check your record while you're locked up. I'd bet the farm he'd find something that would keep you in jail for a while."

Rabbit squirmed a little and looked at Jiffy.

"His brother's name is Troy," Jiffy said, "and he is the law around here, that's for sure. That's why shit-for-brains, here, can get away with shoving people around. Otherwise somebody would bust his chops for sure."

"It won't be you," J.C. said.

Rabbit was silent for a moment. He took a sip of his beer and looked around the saloon. "Where's Blondie? Does she come in here?"

"She knew you were coming so she stayed home," J.C. answered.

"That's bullshit," Jiffy said. "She's at Troy's house watching his baby. She has no idea you're here."

"Go home, Jiffy," J.C. said.

"Fuck you."

"Here we go again."

"She's watching the cop brother's kid?" Rabbit asked.

"His wife's missing and he's up in the mountains looking for her, where J.C. would be if he were any kind of brother," Jiffy answered. "She fell off her horse or some shit and now they can't find her."

"So he's not even around?"

"Go home, Jiffy," J.C. repeated.

"Fuck you, J.C."

"You guys are a fucking ball," Rabbit said.

"You can go home, too," J.C. said.

"I see you still go by the name, J.C.," Rabbit said. "Do you still think you shoot pool like Jesus Christ, or do you just keep the name to impress people?"

"I'm good enough."

"Sure he can still beat most of the fish in town," Jiffy said. "But I've seen more than one road player take him down a notch or two."

"Tell you what, then," Rabbit said. "I always wanted to get even with you for the bad beat you gave me in California years ago. Let's play Nine Ball. I'd say a run to six or seven games should do it. If I lose, I'll walk away."

"I'm not playing you pool for my wife. Now who's the dumbass? Dumbass."

"You wouldn't exactly be playing *for* her," Jiffy quickly said, again adding his two-cents worth to the conversation. "What you'll be playing for is whether or not Rabbit, here, will be allowed to talk to her without interference."

"Right," Rabbit said and tipped his glass to Jiffy. "Anyway, women like it when men fight over them."

"Ain't going to happen," J.C. said.

"Maybe you could get your boy to play for you, if you're chicken shit," Rabbit said. "I understand that's what you did last time you set up a big game because you let old age and booze rob you of any ability you ever had. Jesus Christ, my ass. More like Jiminy Cricket."

Rabbit glanced at Jiffy and they both laughed.

J.C. closed his eyes and fought the urge to crack both over the head with . . . with what? He had nothing but his two old and weak fists. But truth was truth. He was shaky at best, and old age and bad eyes had robbed him of a good part of the game he once possessed. And he couldn't bear the thought of Blondie leaving him again and maybe taking Kid with her. That would be devastating. He regretted all the years of not telling her how he really felt about her. And truth being truth, he loved her very much. "I haven't played for anything substantial in years," he said, "just a few sawbucks here and there. And as true as it is that Kid is a world-beater, a hell of a lot better than me or you, it wouldn't take anyone with that much talent to beat you, I'm sure." J.C. realized he was still talking trash after all these years even though he was pretty sure he might have trouble backing it up against this earring wearing sissy.

"If you lose, then," Rabbit said, "you'll let me approach her without your fucking cop brother hassling me, right?"

"I didn't say we were going to play. But if we did and I lose, you're only to see what she wants to do. And that's all you'll do," J.C. said. "But if I win, you'll walk away and leave her and me alone. Is that the deal?"

"Right," Rabbit answered, "right."

Jiffy was out of his seat and immediately busting through the door.

"Where the fuck's he going so fast?" Rabbit watched through the window as the old house painter skipped down the street.

"To spread the word all over town that my dad's an idiot," Kid said, now standing behind his father shaking his head disapprovingly, "and that he's going to play a game of pool for his wife. "And if you lose—" he looked his father in the eye "—I'm going with her."

"Don't be so high and mighty, son," J.C. said. "If you had half a chance, you'd play him for any stake, and you know it. And I'd back you too."

"True," Kid said. "In a minute, and I'd beat him for sure."

Rabbit laughed. "We have at least one player with some balls in the house, but this is between your chicken-shit father and me. But maybe someday, when you have something worthwhile to play for, you'll get that chance. It might be fun. As for you, old man, just let me know when and where.

***

"Game on! Game on!" Jiffy went running up and down Mesquite Avenue, ducking in and out of each bar and saloon. He hit them all, yukking it up and telling anyone who would listen how J.C. was going to play some pool hustler from California, and that the stakes were his wife, the one who had just come back to him.

And again, pool fever, like gold fever, began to spread around the bar and saloon crowd.

20

Holly stirred again in a dream state; someone was lying beside her. The musky odor filled the air and invoked her emotions. He was so close she could feel his breath on the nape of her neck. She could feel his hands sliding along her thighs, fingers caressing, kneading. She could feel his manhood between her legs, sliding, probing, and she could feel her underpants becoming moist, wet with the anticipation of what was coming, and her legs began to spread involuntarily. She wanted to accept him fully. "Tex," she moaned loudly and the sound of her own voice jarred her awake and in a blink of an eye she saw the Indian, not Tex. She screamed and rolled away from him, but when she hit the wall, no one was lying in bed with her. Instead the Indian was crouched by the fire, painted face smiling at her, his nakedness hanging low to the ground. He was as big as she remembered, in all respects, but now, somehow, he looked gentle, harmless, desirable.

How is it possible, she asked herself, that this bizarre Indian had abducted her, dragged her into his cave, kicked her into silence, and yet she was dreaming of making love to him? "Who are you?" she asked. "Are you real?"

"Am Hoskininni, Chief of All Land," he said.

"What do you want with me?"

"You Ta-ay. You be my woman."

"I'm not Ta-a-a-a." She tried to pronounce the name. "I'm Holly Forkner, woman of the chief of police of Upland."

"Me, *Chief*, Chief of All Land," he yelled and moved instantly toward her. "You Ta-ay. You my woman." He backhanded her across the face.

She reeled backward. Her head struck the rock wall.

Holly wiped the blood from her mouth. Any endearment she might have felt instantly faded.

He turned and pointed to the hanging slivers of dried rodents. "Have food."

Just looking at the dead menagerie made her stomach crawl. "You're fucking kidding me."

He raised his hand and swung. Holly ducked. But the swing caught the back of her head, again knocking her backwards. "Look asshole," she said fighting back tears, "if you expect me to be your woman, you'll have to treat me better than this."

His eyes glided over her, from foot to head, but he said nothing. He only turned and dislodged a piece of meat. "Have squirrel. You eat."

"You expect me to eat that crap—" She bit her tongue trying to stop the words when he looked as if he would retaliate.

But he turned away and set a thin flat rock on the fire. "Cook for you now. Then you always cook for me."

"That's disgusting," Holly said as she watched the sliver of aging meat hit the hot rock, but her stomach growled when it began to sizzle.

There was now six feet or so between them, about the same distance to the exit. She carefully watched him. He was busy tending to his cooking. "Do you live on the reservation or in town?" She asked trying to keep him distracted.

"Live in forest, live in trees, live in wind," he said and stirred the meat with a stick.

"You live in town, I've seen you," she said but was thinking about how close the way out was.

He started for her then stopped, "Am Chief—"

"Yeah, I got it, crazy chief of all the land. But what do you want from me?"

"Chief Hoskininni want you. Red Hawk want you."

Freedom, she decided, was only a quick dash away. She knew she needed to get out any way possible, and there was no time to consider the probability of her outrunning him enough to hide in the woods. Or, if she made it to the river, what would be the likelihood of her out-swimming him?

It did not matter, Holly was up and running. She made it to the exit, sunlight blasting into her eyes. Then suddenly, with a painful snap, her feet yanked out from under her and she hit the dirt with an air-escaping thud.

"Fuck!" she moaned and knew at once that she was tethered to a rock.

"You mine," the Indian yelled as he slid across the dirt floor, seized her by the feet, and flung her back into the cave, like a kid playing with a rag doll. This time, when her head hit the wall, she blinked once and faded into unconsciousness.

21

"So this is it?" Nina asked as Pike parked in front of the Hopi Trading Post. They had reported their findings to the tribal administration and police. From there, they had called Troy to make their report to him also. Then Pike had promised to treat her to the "nation's best breakfast."

The trading post was much larger and modern than Nina had expected, with paved and lighted parking, a tall double-door entrance to the gift shop and restaurant areas, and packed with customers.

"What do you think?"

"Looks like a tourist trap."

"In case somebody wins at the casino," Pike said, "maybe they'll stop here and give it back."

"Impressive," Nina said, though not impressed. "But you didn't drag me out here to show me a building. I remember something about breakfast."

Inside, they took a seat by the window, had barely sat down when a very attractive, though somewhat plump, waitress approached. She had straight black hair, dark eyes, and wore no makeup. Not that she needed it. "Good morning, Pike."

"Morning, Mansi." Pike smiled at the waitress. "Two of my usual, scrambled."

"And coffee," Nina said. "Lots of coffee, my newbie friend here is buying."

"Ooh, Pike, finally a real date—" the waitress grinned "—anything serious?"

"The first of many," Pike said and winked.

"Not on a bet." Nina spoke fast and a little loud. "The rookie has to buy for dragging me all the way out here. It's not a date."

The waitress raised her eyebrows at Nina. "Keep your eye on him, sister. He's only interested in one thing."

"Oh?" Nina said.

"Work, that's it. He's certainly not interested in anything meaningful."

"Okay," Nina said, "good to know."

"What?" Pike questioned, "Now you want something meaningful? How about you and I—"

"Fat chance." The waitress laughed as she walked away.

"What were Troy's plans?" Pike asked Nina in a more serious tone, but he kept his eyes on the waitress as she purposely sashayed toward the kitchen.

"Said he was going to search the area over Squaw Butte by airplane before he makes the money drop," Nina answered. "He thinks he can cover more ground from the air. But I think that if Red Hawk, or Palmer—or whatever the hell his name is—abducted Holly and didn't bring her here, to the reservation, then he might have carried her up to the reservoir, and not over by Squaw Butte. That's just too far and too rugged, unless he had a vehicle waiting for him at the reservoir, a motor home or something. That makes more sense to me. For all we know, Holly might still be up there locked up in one of them with her mouth sewn shut, a la Dean Koontz."

"What?"

"He's an author who . . . never mind."

"Anyway, Palmer doesn't drive," Pike said. "And the neighbor woman said he hangs out around Zuni Wells and Shadow Mountain."

"Maybe he had an accomplice who does drive."

The waitress set two plates in front of them. Eggs with wild mushrooms and chunks of green vegetables scrambled in, thick-cut pan-fried potatoes, and sizzling ground meat covered with red and green peppers.

"Puke and hamburger for breakfast," Nina said.

The waitress smiled at her.

"Hamburger? Okay." Pike smiled. "It's—"

"Wait, don't tell me," Nina said. "It does smell fantastic and, no matter what it is, if you can eat it, so can I." She slid from her seat. "But let me go to the little girl's room first, and then we'll dig in."

"It's getting cold." Pike protested.

"Won't be a minute."

On her way back from the bathroom, Nina was enjoying the quaint interior of a building efficiently built to relieve the throng of tourists from the bankrolls they were willing to relinquish for a taste of *real* Indian culture, though the place couldn't be any farther away from Hopi culture if it were in New York City. When she turned the corner of a row of booths, thinking about eating buffalo, rattlesnake, opossum, road kill, or whatever Pike had brought her here for, she stopped, dead still. "Son of a bitch," she said under her breath. Tucked behind and well hidden by the plants in a room divider, Palmer—she was sure it was him—was eating breakfast, a normal breakfast like a normal person, which, in itself, shocked her. Though he wore the same filthy clothing she'd seen him in the day before, his hands were clean, and he was using a knife and fork. He carefully buttered his toast, set it aside, cut a slice from his ham steak, and laid the knife down before eating. All completely out of character from what she had envisioned from him, just like the clean one-room building he lived in.

She slowly maneuvered herself behind a rack of Arizona post cards and back to Pike's table.

"Pike, he's here," she whispered.

"Who's here?"

"The Indian, Mark Palmer," Nina continued to whisper and motioned for Pike to do the same.

"Bull," Pike also whispered but wasn't sure why. "If he's expecting the ransom money today, why would he be here?"

"He can retrieve the money anytime he chooses," Nina said.

"He doesn't drive."

"I heard," Nina said. "Let's take him in." She didn't wait for a response and started back around the planter.

Pike looked at his plate and frowned. "Damn!" he mumbled as jumped up, and followed her.

"Palmer, we need to talk to you." Nina stepped in front of his table.

Mose Duane

Palmer looked up but did not respond.

"I want to ask you a couple of questions," Nina said.

At that moment, the waitress came around the corner with two steaming cups of coffee.

Palmer's eyes shifted from Nina to the waitress. He stood and pulled a hunting knife from his belt.

"What are you doing?" Nina asked. She eased her hand to her pistol grip.

Palmer raised the knife, turned from the waitress and pointed it at Nina.

"Hey, cousin," Pike said, "This is a good time to talk, enit? You don't need the knife. She just wants to ask you a couple of questions."

Palmer looked at Pike, a hint of recognition crossed his face, and he slowly slipped the knife into its sheath but kept his hand on the handle.

"Mark, that's your name, right?" Nina moved slowly toward him. "I need you to tell me about the book we found in your house."

Palmer looked perplexed.

"It's a book about Indian spirits."

"The spirit took her, I told you that. It was the spirit, not Red Hawk. He took the woman Holly. He hid her."

"Right, I remember." Nina moved her hand from her pistol and held it out to show she was no threat.

"Did the spirit take her for you?" Pike asked.

"Do you know where she is?" Nina asked and Palmer bolted for her, his head low.

She fumbled getting to her pistol and pushed it into the air as she took Palmer's advance solidly in the gut. The pistol discharged as she flew backward across a table, disrupting two diners.

The wayward shot missed the waitress by mere inches. "Oh shit! Oh shit!" she muttered, holding the two cups of steaming coffee. Patrons dove for cover.

Palmer scrambled for the door, but like a linebacker, Pike dove and knocked him to his knees. "Don't run man, we just want to talk."

Palmer grabbed Pike by the neck and flung him into the counter. Water glasses, cups, and saucers crashed to the floor.

Nina pulled herself up, but Palmer was there swinging. His left fist caught her in the head, knocking her between two tables.

"Oh shit! Oh shit!" the waitress repeated.

Pike was up, and again dove at Palmer "God damn it, cousin, be sensible." He wrapped his arms around the Indian's neck, trying to keep him on the floor, but one heave sent Pike flying backward across the display of postcards, scattering pictures of cactus and jackalopes across the floor.

Palmer staggered to his feet.

Nina grasped two chairs for leverage and lunged at Palmer, tackled him around the ankles tripping him back to the floor. This time, before the Indian could recover, Nina shoved the barrel of her pistol two inches into the wild man's mouth. "I said I wanted to talk to you, goddamn it."

Lightning fast, Palmer's fist slammed into Nina's jaw, sending her upward and backward. The pistol pulled right and discharged again, splintering the wood floor beside the Indian's head. He spun and kicked, sending

Nina sailing across another table, scattering chairs, food, and two old men who were hunkered beneath the table.

"Oh shit! Oh shit!" the waitress intoned, bouncing up and down behind the counter, still holding the coffees, trying her damnedest not to spill any, and not having the rational wherewithal to take cover.

Pike scrambled to retrieve Nina's pistol, leveled it and fired twice as Palmer hurled himself out the front door.

Nina and Pike chased Palmer across the street where he ducked into a mess of palo verde and piñon trees. Once within the thicket, he vanished.

"Damn it!" Nina yelled. "How could you miss him going out the door?"

"Me?" Pike said, his voice stressed. "You're the one who had a pistol in his mouth, and still missed. How lame was that?"

Nina just grinned, big and bold. Her heart pounded wildly. "Hell, I just wanted to talk to him," she said and they both laughed.

Back inside, they ate their mystery breakfast while the staff cleaned up the mess of broken dishes and upturned tables. Then, two tribal police officers, both friends of Pike's, spent more time teasing Nina about her choice of breakfast and company than they did filling out their incident report.

Nina argued that she was there on official business only, so whom she was with didn't matter, and she refused to concede the breakfast to be the nation's best, but had to admit that both the company and the food were unique.

22

Beth McDonald had just climbed the flight of stairs to the control tower at the Upland airport. She turned on the outdated equipment to give it time to warm up. The airport was fully operational only in the daytime, and being one of only three contract controllers working for the city, she usually took the morning shift.

While waiting, she scanned the sky and saw no traffic in the pattern. But when she checked the tarmac for ground activity, she saw Troy's beautiful yellow Waco taxiing toward the runway.

"Morning, Troy." She spoke into the radio mike.

"Morning, Beth," Troy responded. "I saw the lights come on in the tower and was waiting for your friendly voice."

"How are you this morning? Sorry to hear about Holly, have you found her yet?"

"Not yet. I'm going up now to drop the ransom money."

"Cleared for takeoff," Beth immediately said. "Good luck."

"Cleared." Troy repeated and pegged the throttle. The canary-yellow airplane rumbled down the runway, rose just enough to clear the tree tops, and leveled off there.

Beth still loved Troy and had finally admitted it to herself after all this time. Her knees weakened and her face flushed every time she cleared him for take off or landing. Two years ago, citing some noble cause of not wanting to come between him and Holly, she had passed up her opportunity with him before he married. She now regretted not pursuing him at that time, and fleetingly wondered what her chances would be if Holly wasn't found, but quickly rejected the thought as callous. Then just as quickly, she changed her mind. Everyone in town knew Holly wasn't happy here, she reasoned, and that made Troy miserable and her heart bled for him. And she would do whatever she could to comfort him.

"Holler at me when you get back and I'll buy you a cup of coffee," she said into her mike before his plane disappeared over the forest.

"We haven't done that in a long time," Troy answered. "Sounds like fun."

***

As Troy kept the aircraft low, skimming barely ten feet above the highest tree branches, he thought about Beth. She was a beautiful girl with long curly blond hair, deep blue eyes, and a bright smile that always knocked his socks off. And they had a lot in common. Like him, she was trained in the Air Force and loved to be around airplanes. He thought that to be a rare thing to find in a gorgeous woman. But he knew that he would never call her. His love for Holly would prevent that no matter what the future brought. He would never replace Holly.

In slow flight the bi-winged Waco could fly an achingly dawdling forty knots without stalling. But even if it were to stall, a subtle forward push of the stick to lower the nose would recover it instantly. The plane could practically fly itself, which meant he could spend ninety-nine percent of his time looking overboard for anything that appeared out of place.

He had deliberately mentioned the ransom drop to Beth in case the kidnapper was keeping tabs on him. Anyone with a transceiver could pick up his transmission and the kidnapper certainly knew he had an airplane. Troy figured the guy surely would be smart enough to listen in and wanted him to know the drop was on track.

He was well ahead of schedule and could cover a lot of territory before making the drop. He knew the quirks of updrafts and downdrafts while flying low and slow over the national forest as well as anyone; he'd flown over it hundreds of times, mostly alone but also many hours with Holly. He knew where the rivers and streams converged, where tree-cover hid the flowing waterways and where an individual could take refuge. But, if he flew low enough and slow enough, maybe he could see signs of an out-of-place camp, campfire, tent, or vehicle where someone could hole up, even if it had not been used for some time. If he found anything suspicious, he'd mark the coordinates on his aeronautical chart and check it out when he got back on the ground.

Troy burned time and fuel zigzagging across the myriad fire roads, dry washes, and trickling streams leading to and from the reservoir and the two rivers that fed it, hoping that whoever had taken Holly would have stayed close to the water. But he found nothing that looked out of the ordinary.

Finally, with time running out, he turned toward Squaw Butte, a spike of dirt covered rock with sparse foliage that pointed skyward out of the dense ponderosa east of Shadow Mountain. Scattered around the butte were several Indian ruins and burial grounds overrun by whites who saw them only as mounds, but still sacred to many Indians. Troy put the Waco into a tight turn to make a full circle, and went around twice. He saw no one and nothing looked out of the ordinary so, on the third pass, he rolled the plane upside down and let the backpack fall from the front seat. It barely cleared the top wing, but he was in no jeopardy of it hitting him or the stabilizers as it rapidly slid beneath his head and tumbled earthward.

Troy made a quick, tight loop around the knob and never took his eyes off the bag until it disappeared into the treetops. He circled one more time, and as he passed over the drop area, he toggled a switch on a small transceiver to activate a micro transmitter clipped onto a seam of the backpack. When the bag moved, he'd know it. He lowered the nose of the Waco and continued his meandering search until just prior to dark, then plotted a direct heading for the Rim Airpark where he would put down for the night. He'd stay there in his log cabin at the airpark where he would be as close to Squaw Butte as possible while waiting for a signal from the bag.

That night, while laying in the bed he and Holly had made into their love nest, he vowed never to let work get between him and his family. Holly and Jesse would be the center of his universe from this point on. Brother

J.C. was absolutely right: Family first. But he realized that it may have already been too late.

23

J.C. and Kid found their favorite bench in Town Square Park across the street from the saloon. The bench was beneath the limbs of a massive oak that swayed and whipped as the wind eddied through it. As usual, the park was full. Both locals and flatlanders up from Phoenix escaping the heat liked to bask in the laidback lifestyle watching squirrels scurry up and down tree trunks and listening to birds twitter their summer warbles.

"Love this place," J.C. said as he stretched his legs out in front of the bench and fumbled for a cigarette.

"What's the story with Rabbit?" Kid asked as soon as he also settled in, as if he couldn't contain the question any longer.

J.C. stopped shuffling from pocket to pocket when he remembered he had not smoked for almost two years. "A devil's tool," he said, "a coffin's nail, one of the banes of life, son, I know. But I still miss the damn things."

"You don't need them," Kid said. "Don't even think about them."

J.C. put his hands behind his head and leaned back, more to give his fingers something to do than for comfort. "About ten or twelve years ago," he said, "I beat Rabbit out of every dime he owned in a marathon Nine Ball game that lasted fourteen hours non-stop. A few years after that, he began hanging around Johnny Bishop's pool hall where I worked in California thinking he was going to get his money back, but never came close."

"I remember Johnny!" Kid said. "And Black Berry, he was shot right over there—" Kid pointed to the parking space where Black Berry died.

"Right and you remembered Rabbit from back then too."

"Sure, he and mom stole all of Black Berry's pool cues, sold them, and took the money on the road. You then blew up Johnny's safe because it had Black Berry's money in it. Then you bashed him over the head with your Rambow cue. Then we came here, trying to hide from him. I remember all that."

"Right again."

"But Black Berry found us anyway," Kid said, "and the Mexicans found him here too, and shot him because the money was really theirs."

"But all that's not important to our conversation about Rabbit. What you don't know is that he's a slick talker, as smooth as a young lady's butt, I'd say, and he wooed your mother with promises of a glamorous life on the road shooting pool and winning big tournaments up in Chicago. Blondie had the game and the stroke, as you well know. She could hold her own against most players. But Rabbit proved not to be the best partner for her, at least at that time. So, now she's here."

"And so is he," Kid said. "Were they lovers?"

"I'm sure your mother, like most of us, has done things that she's not proud of."

"You said I was old enough to know the truth."

"I'm telling you the truth, son, as I know it. But if I had to venture a guess, I'd say yes, probably, no doubt. Hell, maybe she's proud of it, I don't know. Nonetheless, that doesn't matter at all, not to me. What does matter is that I figure there's only one person in town that could beat Rabbit in a straight up, normal Nine Ball game."

"I'm not going to play him for my mother," Kid said.

J.C. laughed. "You think I'm talking about *you* beating him?"

"Who else?" Kid shrugged his shoulders and flashed a cocky smile. "I'm as sure as hell that it's not you."

"Ah, son, I can remember a time when I was the audacious one, the world beater who could thrash anyone on a pool table and knew it. Anyway, Rabbit already said he wouldn't play you in this instance, though I'd say we could probably hound him into it if we tried hard enough. But we're not going to, even if I don't think I can beat him in a straight up game. But there may be another way."

"There's always another way with you."

"Yes it's a fact, and as I recall, Rabbit tends to lose his concentration after several hours of play and doesn't realize it's happening. So I'm thinking that maybe I can use that to my advantage."

"Hmmm," Kid said. "I'm listening."

"There's a lesson to be learned here too, son," J.C. answered. "It's a good thing to know you opponent's weakness before you play him."

"So you've told me, maybe a hundred times."

"Only a hundred?"

"Maybe more," Kid said and laughed.

"Probably so, and don't you forget it. In Rabbit's case, though, I think it's like driving when you're a little drunk. You actually think you're a better driver than when you're sober, though it's far from true. So, when Rabbit gets tired, he's subject to think he's a better player than he really is, and he takes chances that he wouldn't normally take. The way I see it, I have to get him into a long, drawn-out game and outlast him, exploit his weakness you might say."

"He wants to play a run to seven or something," Kid said. "That won't last more than a couple of hours at most, and that's if you drag it out."

"That's true. But, like everyone else, he's not as young as he used to be and I'd bet a silver dime to a doughnut hole that he can only make it three or four hours, tops, before his mind starts to wander. I've seen him lose a lot of games because he refuses to stop when he's ahead, and that's when we were young."

Kid mulled that for a moment. "Here's a silly notion," he said. "Why don't you just ask mom what her intentions are? Then there won't be any need for playing him."

J.C. jumped as if a bolt of electricity had hit him. "Christ O Mighty, son, I thought you understood. I can't take that chance. I mean, look at the three of us, for Christ's sake." J.C. settled back into his seat and squirmed a little. "Rabbit's younger than me and nice looking too, I guess . . . for a pussy hippie anyway. And your mother's still young too, and beautiful I might add. And, hell, I'm almost twenty years older. I'm worn out and dragging a foot in the grave. I'm not so lame as to think that I have a chance if we give her the option to choose, unless it's eeny meeny miny moe or some such shit. No, I've got to win this game without her knowing about it. I've got to get rid of Rabbit, and not give her the choice. I don't even want her to know he's in town if I can prevent it." J.C., now misty-eyed, looked away from Kid. "Christ, son, I can't take the chance."

"It's not the right thing to do," Kid said.

J.C. twisted his mouth trying to absorb what Kid was saying. "Has nothing to do with right or wrong. It has to do with playing to win. I've always managed to bend the rules in my favor just for that reason, son, I play to win. And that's all I'm doing here, bending a few rules to win one last game."

Kid thought about it for a moment. "I don't want mom to leave either, but I think it should be up to her, without any tricks. And, if she finds out that you played Nine Ball for her, Christ, she's going to be pissed at both of us and will probably leave anyway, no matter the outcome of the game."

"I know you're right, son. But I just can't take the chance. I couldn't bear for her to choose him over me again. Son, I couldn't bear to lose her again now that she's here. If we just go do it and get it over with, I think we can pull it off and she'll never know."

"No," Kid said. "I've thought it over and I don't want any part of your shenanigans. But I won't tell mom either. I'll play dumb and leave it up to you and your conscience."

"What if I told you this really has nothing to do with your mother? That it's really a game that's between me and him. A game that's been brewing for a long time."

"Don't try to con me, I know better . . . but then again, there is a lot of truth to that. You think you have to beat him one last time, one last game, like you said. And I understand that with you, there has to be something *substantial* to play for. What I don't understand is why you guys can't just go play."

"That's hooey, son. Of course you understand. Now that you're a player, you'll never again play unless there's something substantial at stake."

"Okay, that's probably true, but leave me out of this one."

"Probably? You know it's true, son. You'd give up just about anything to play this game."

Kid mulled that over for a moment. "Just remember this, you get tired just as easily as Rabbit does and if you go to sleep on your feet, you're screwed."

"I know that son, that's why I need you. It'll be your job—and it's an important job too—to keep me focused and awake."

"You'll have to do it on your own somehow," Kid said. "It just doesn't feel right. It feels like I'm betraying my own mother."

"Yeah, I suppose you're right. I suppose this one's on me, by myself, and if it does go south, I certainly wouldn't want to drag you down any shit holes with me."

"Now that that's settled, what's the plan?"

J.C. eyed Kid for a moment and smiled. "I'll approach him when he's buying his new entourage beers and tell him that I don't want any of this wham-bam, thank-you-ma'am pussy pool. That it has to be a man's game."

"A man's game?"

"Sure, a game of endurance is what I'll tell him. I'll tell him it has to last six or seven hours."

Kid made a face and raised his eyebrows. "Sounds plausible, think he'll go for it?"

"He already thinks that I think he's a sissy. He'll go for it to show all of his new fans that he's not."

"Always the schemer," Kid said. "Is there another lesson to be learned in there somewhere?"

J.C. laughed, grabbed Kid on the knee and squeezed. "Come on, son, and I'll let you buy me another soda pop."

24

By the time Nina and Pike got back to Upland it was well into the afternoon so they agreed to go home for the rest of the day, get a good night's sleep, meet at the Downtown diner for an early "real" breakfast, then split up. Nina would check out the reservoir and Pike would drive to Shadow Mountain or, more specifically, Zuni Wells, which was located below the mountain.

Before going home, Nina checked out the new construction site. The building was coming along superbly; the outside brickwork was almost complete, down to mostly cleanup. The interior drywall and paint were done, with trim and baseboards going in. She drifted past what was going to be the reception desk, down a hallway to a room designated to be her office. She leaned against the doorjamb to envision her decorating plans. But her mind wandered and she again began thinking of Troy. What if?—She stopped herself in mid-thought, and felt ashamed. But, damn it, what if Holly didn't come back? Was she supposed to ignore her own feelings? Was she supposed to sit on the sidelines and watch some other woman help Troy through his grieving? And what about Pike?

"Damn it." This time she said it aloud and scratched at her nose. Holly had to be alive and she'd do everything in her power to help find her. And if Palmer was their perpetrator, he had to have had a partner. There was no way he acted alone and the more she thought about it, the more she believed in her motor home theory. It would be so easy to hide in plain sight at the reservoir.

Nina left the construction site and drove to the station to check in.

"Anything?" she asked Duke, who was holding down the fort alone.

"Nothing," Duke answered. Then spying over his glasses and smiling broadly he added, "I thought you were going home with Pike?"

"Pike's going to his house, and I'm going to mine," Nina said and sighed.

"Yeah, that's what I meant." Duke corrected himself, but continued to smile.

Nina looked around the small cramped room that had been the Upland police headquarters for as long as she could remember and decided she did not want to be there either.

"See ya," she said abruptly, then turned for the door.

"Yep," Duke said as he watched the door slam shut. "You got it bad."

Nina drove home, ran a bath and soaked her weary, frustrated self. The water was warm and soothing. And then there *is* Pike, Nina thought about what Duke had teasingly said and smiled. Though not classically handsome like Troy, Pike looked good, tall, broad-shouldered, and muscular. But his nose was too big, his mouth too small, and his eyebrows too bushy. He was not her type.

Pike, on the other hand, went straight home. He brewed his tea, stripped out of his uniform, and settled in for a relaxing afternoon in the sweat lodge pondering the man who called himself Red Hawk. He had a day's head start and, if the old woman living next door to him was right, he would not return to his house but would be well on his way to Zuni Wells to do whatever he did there. Once he finished that, he would then disappear into the forest and Pike could take days finding him. It made sense to Pike that he might have better luck tracking Palmer down at Zuni Wells at night, and tonight would be the most logical, when Palmer least expected it.

Not really wanting to leave the comfort of his sweat lodge, Pike rejected his uniform and reluctantly stepped back into his civvies. He then packed his Corvette with the few supplies he thought he would need. He was sure a full night among the dark spirits of the burial grounds at Zuni Wells would be challenging, but it also would be a good place for a sane Indian to track down a crazy one.

Though the town council had not yet allowed him a patrol car or pistol, he was thankful they saw fit to supply him with a handheld radio, which he made sure was fully charged, but turned off in case Nina or Troy got some last minute idea about reassigning him to the night shift. He also strapped his hunting knife to his right hip as his only weapon. He thought about taking his personal .32 but, because of department regs, rejected the idea.

On Highway 89, several miles past the rutted trail Nina had taken along the river at Verde River Bridge, Pike turned west toward the mountain. For two solid hours, he meandered along several neglected dirt roads and trails going west then south before circling back west toward the mountain. Pike figured that even with Palmer's head start and direct cross-country march they should arrive at the lake at about the same time and well before dark. Which would be perfect since Pike couldn't do anything until after dark anyway.

At the lake, Pike eased the Corvette off the long, straight access road that paralleled the lake and parked on the packed caliche, at the water's edge.

Zuni Wells was a collection of springs that filled with rain and snowmelt runoff from Shadow Mountain during the winter months to form a small lake, and an underground aquifer fed the springs during the summer months, though at a much slower rate. The lake, an oasis in the flat desert valley at the base of the mountain, even with its sparse vegetation, stood out in stark contrast to the dry rolling foothills, mesas, and knobs of land that made up the surrounding territory. Natives and wildlife had used the lake as a watering hole for hundreds of years, and now shared it with hardy campers and fishermen. Though smaller than the Upland reservoir, the lake was much larger than Pike had expected.

In an attempt to appear to be there fishing, Pike unpacked his camping gear and set up a small camp between the automobile and the lake, while waiting for nightfall. Across the lake, where the ground was wet year round, thick vegetation only slightly obscured three campsites, and Pike wondered if Palmer's was one of them. But Palmer probably would not have a typical campsite that close to the water. Pike made a mental note as to where the camps were located anyway.

Waiting for the sun to submerge below the peaks of the mountain, Pike fumbled with a fishing line for a few minutes with the notion that he would blend in better if he actually had a hook in the water. Also, the thought of catching a small chub for dinner while doing so excited him a little because he hadn't done any kind of fishing in years. Chubs weren't the best eating fish in Arizona but they'd do in a pinch and they were easy to catch. However, he soon rejected the idea as too awkward and time consuming and let the now-tangled line drift in the water. Passing on the fishing gave him the time to build a campfire to brew tea, a more worthy cause, he figured. While the tea was brewing, he sat on his plush sleeping roll and popped open a can of pork-n-beans.

The thought of his ancestors looking down from above to watch him eat from a can while sitting in comfort bothered him. They would be making faces and shaking their heads wondering if he was truly one of their descendents. But he was, he assured himself. Though more assimilated into the white man's culture than most Navajos he knew, he could never deny where he came from. He raised a palm-forward hand toward the heavens in a symbolic gesture to assure the sun god *Tsohanoai,* who may at this moment be questioning his continuing faith, that he had not faltered.

In that respect, Pike figured that he and Nina were a lot alike. He would never want her to reject her roots, but, on the other hand, she was no inner-city native who refused to learn proper English or become part of the American culture into which she was born. Pike and Nina were modern people, undeniably linked to a different ancient culture, but not anchored by some belief that they had been irrevocably wronged by society either. That gave them something else in common, and Pike liked the thought of having something in common with Nina.

Sipping his tea, Pike watched the pale mauve sunset over Juniper Mountain far to the west, accentuated by a few ballooning clouds coming in from the north. Pinholes of light were appearing in the darkening sky to the east, each pinhole representing the center of a universe, and he thought about the smallness and pettiness of his own existence in the great scheme of the world. "Are these the thoughts of a true Indian?" He again questioned his heritage, but his answer was sure, why not? And, since he was thinking of the great scheme of things, he had no bona fide way of knowing what really might be lurking about this sacred ground of the long dead. On the one hand, he told himself how modern he was, but, on the other hand, he still got the eerie feeling that he was not alone, especially out here. Call them shadows or ghosts or spirits or whatever, he was always aware of their presence, watching, judging, evaluating. Again he held up a hand to the sky. "Peace," he said.

25

Red Hawk had made the journey across the mountain to Zuni Wells in record time, and standing on a knoll west of the lake, he'd watched the red and white car turn off the road and park by the water. He'd seen the car before and knew it was the Navajo policeman who drove it. He did not hate the Navajo policeman as much as he hated the white policemen.

He had not returned to his place on the reservation. He would never go there again. From this time on, his place would be in the mountain forest with the woman Holly. He would become the Indian he always wanted to be, an Indian in the mold of his ancestors. With the woman, he would start anew.

He now sat cross-legged facing a small flickering fire. But this time he sat between two burial mounds containing the remains of Indian warriors of the past, one of which he believed to be the great warrior Hoskininni. Red Hawk had been there before, in that exact spot doing that exact thing. Days ago, he had called upon the spirit of Hoskininni to capture the woman Holly for him, and to take her to the stronghold where no one could find her. That day at the river, together Red Hawk and Hoskininni had taken her and hauled her away. It was dreamlike and vague in his mind; and so sporadic was his recollection that there were gaps in his memory as to all that had happened. They had carried her along the river, had hidden her, and Red Hawk could not recall where. Only the spirit of Hoskininni could find her again.

As Red Hawk puffed on his pipe of marijuana leaves and peyote juice, he pulled trinkets—smooth pitch-black river pebbles, turquoise nuggets, sulfur dust, pollen, and human bone slivers dug from the nearby graves of his ancestors—from his doeskin pouch and showered them over the fire. Instantly chutes of pure blue flame shrouded in brilliant yellow sparkles burst into the air. He began chanting the only mantra he'd learned, the one he'd always used, "I hey yea yea. I hey yea yea. I hey yea yea." Over and over he recited the words as he waved his hand across the flame. His cadence was perfect, his sing-song hypnotic.

The wind whistled through the thick foliage and over the folds of the earth where the ancients were buried. The conjuring was easy this time. It was becoming easier with each calling. And again, the powerful spirit of Hoskininni came to him. Red Hawk could see him and talk to him and was assured that together they would become as the Aztec were, as the Zuni were, as the Pueblo were, uncontaminated by whites, and together they would have the woman Holly.

And the policeman by the lake would be taken care of.

26

Pike waited, his mind wandering between the mystic, the real, and Nina, until only a sliver of a moon and a million stars peeked through scattered clouds and softly lit the night. Then he went hunting. Slowly and silently, and keeping with the old ways of the Navajo, he crept south around the lake staying low within the undergrowth. He slipped in and out of countless jetties and waterways looking for any sign of his quarry; this would be the time to catch him off guard, maybe even asleep.

On the south side of the lake, Pike found the campsites he'd seen earlier from across the lake. Covertly, he moved in and out of each site leaving campers blissfully unaware that an Indian was creeping within the shadows of their camps. Finding nothing there, he continued around the lake to the burial grounds, defined by the seemingly random placement of rocks and mounds over a hundred years earlier.

Deliberately and quietly, Pike crept well into the interior of the place revered by Indians and no one else until what he found came as no surprise. Kneeling behind a smoldering fire, Palmer was sifting a handful of fine sand and dirt across the embers in what looked like the finishing ritual of a Witchery Way. This process was to cover whatever he'd used to lure the spirits to him, especially any human bone fragments. As part of the ritual, those must be returned to Mother Earth.

Modern Pike did not particularly like to admit that he believed in the witching process, not to the extent that many Navajos did anyway, and the old Navajo woman had not liked Palmer's performance, but to Pike, Palmer looked proficient and precise as he performed his finishing ceremony.

And if Palmer was finishing, Pike had to hurry. He swiftly ducked behind a small ridge and moved along a shallow wash that circled Palmer. Then, with his knife drawn, he came up and out of the wash and rushed Palmer's position, only to find that he was too late. Palmer had vanished.

Not wanting to upset the natural order of the spiritual world, Pike did not touch or move any part of Palmer's altar, and especially gave the fire pit a wide berth as he looked for a trail. Palmer had, however, disappeared without leaving so much as a footprint.

Vowing to try again at daybreak, Pike gave up the hunt for the night, completed his circle around the lake, and back to the Corvette. He rekindled his campfire, brewed another cup of tea, leaned back on the vehicle, and sipped the strong brew. The desert heat had escaped into the night sky, but the fire and tea warmed and relaxed him, and he replaced the grim thoughts of Palmer with pleasant ones of Nina. He could see her tall and lean, and he tried to visualize her without her uniform, and wondered if she was completely shaved as an up-to-the-minute contemporary woman might be, or if she was all-natural, as a Navajo woman would be. And before he closed his eyes, with a smile on his face, he pledged to tell her how he felt about her, and maybe find out for himself.

27

This time when Holly's eyes popped open the Indian was squatting beside her, his face only inches from hers. She flinched but did not scream, thinking she was dreaming again and he would move without moving, or simply vanish. But she was not dreaming, nor did he move. She saw his face clearly for the first time. The black and white hue looked more like pigmented skin than paint and it wasn't disconcerting smears as before, but a careful zigzag pattern, stretching back and forth across his face from his forehead down to his neck. His deep black soothing eyes were incredibly alluring and made him seem gentle and harmless. Maybe he wasn't the same Indian. And there was no strong body odor, only the faint musky, feral smell that pleased her senses. Again, her betraying eyes diverted downward where his genitals hung low. Maybe he wasn't even Indian. Maybe he wasn't even real. She wondered if, like a ghost dance in the night, he'd had his way with her while she slept.

Her eyes darted back to his. "Are you real?" she asked.

He looked puzzled.

"Are you a ghost?"

136

"You, me, last true blood." His tranquilizing, irresistible eyes scanned her from head to toe.

"I'm not Indian. Not full-blooded anyway."

"You pure, like me," he snapped. His demeanor changed instantly and his face turned gruff. "You Ta-ay, woman of Chief of All Land."

"You're crazy, unlike me," Holly said as she again glanced at his nakedness. "Did you rape me?"

He stared hard at her. He did not have to speak. She could see lust in his eyes. "So you haven't. Not yet anyway," she said, "but you certainly want to."

He continued to stare, but said nothing.

"Why not? Holly rolled to her side and sat up. "What are you waiting for?"

Still, he did not speak.

"Because," Holly said. "Because you want me to do it willingly, is that it? For whatever reason, I have to participate. That's it. Whatever the hell it is with you, you can't do anything unless I participate."

"You Ta-ay, my woman."

"Well, it ain't going to happen, if that's what you fucking think. If you want me you're going to have to take me."

"I see you look at me," He bellowed, stood, and presented himself.

And she looked again. It was long and growing, a Satyr's erection, stretched and thick, its hefty head pushing through uncircumcised foreskin. Her thoughts wandered. Maybe it was the only way out. Maybe he would let her go or at least let her live if she cooperated. Maybe . . . but at that second, a beam of dim moonlight caught her eye as it flashed between his legs. The diffused light washed through the uncovered exit, bathing the cave in a dull but clear light. She could also hear the river, it sounded close. She'd been so focused on the Indian that she hadn't noticed, and suddenly it gave her hope.

Deftly and silently, with the pointed toe of her boot, she pushed at the rope that tethered her other foot to the rock. The loop was only a precautionary restraint that wasn't tight and, after several pushes, it slipped under the boot's heel, past the snip of the toe, and fell free.

The Indian was standing in an awkward manner, slightly rocking back on his heels, proud of what he was revealing. She made a fist and, without further thought, swung with all the weight she could muster from her sitting position. Her fist caught him solidly on the end of his swollen organ.

The strike sent him sprawling backwards onto the open fire pit, trapping hot rocks and bright embers beneath him. His skin sizzled and his wail was deafening as he tried to recover.

"You're goddamn crazy," Holly screamed and ran like hell.

Though the dull night light stung her eyes, she could see a flat riverbed of rocks leading directly to the river. She had envisioned a high riverbank to dive from, or a forest of trees to dodge into, not this expanse of river rock. But there were numerous tall and dense mounds of driftwood and debris lodged in brush trees scattered along the curve of the riverbank, left by receding water from years of flooding. At the water's edge, she picked up a hand-sized rock, frantically threw it as far into the water as she could, and ducked behind one of the mounds of debris just as the Indian appeared at the river's edge.

He saw the ripples in the water and dove in.

Holly immediately crawled across the river rock to a second pile of debris, and from there headed back toward the cave, the last place he would look for her, she reasoned. At the cave she turned upriver and hugged the cliff as she ran in the opposite direction of where he was looking. She found another dense cluster of driftwood and trees, burrowed beneath it, covered herself with sand and rocks as best she could and, stifling her wild breathing, she waited for daylight.

28

Nina had awakened well before sunrise and had waited for Pike at the Downtown Diner for almost an hour. Then, after calling him several off-colored names, she decided to phone, but he had no phone and that annoyed her even more. She tried his radio, the one he slept with according to him, but he must have turned it off. Fuming, she called Troy thinking that maybe he would meet her for breakfast or at least coffee. But Blondie answered the phone. Not only did Nina wake Blondie and the baby, Troy wasn't home and had not been there all night. "Men," she said to Blondie by way of apology, "you can't depend on any of them."

She left the diner in a huff, and tried Pike again, this time using the cruiser's radio. She hated being stood up, even if it was business. "He'll pay for this," she mumbled. Again into the mike, "Pike, this is Nina, over."

Nothing.

"Pike this is Nina, do you copy, over." Nina fiercely scratched at her nose.

"Nina this is Duke, I'm at the station. You sound perturbed, is everything okay? Over"

"Duke, have you seen or heard from Pike?" she snapped.

"Nope, been here all night, haven't heard a peep from anyone. When can I go home?"

"Call Joe to relieve you, if you can find him," Nina said and slammed the mike onto its hook. Irritated at her thoughts of Troy and at Pike for not answering her calls, she turned the cruiser north, tires squealing, on her way out of town toward the reservoir. "To hell with Pike," she mumbled. She would at least do her part, and if she found Palmer she would either arrest him or shoot him on her own, "to hell with backup." Palmer could be armed and dangerous and was much stronger than one would think. He had already pulled a knife on her and fought like a madman to get away so she sure as hell would shoot him, maybe even on sight. And right now that didn't bother her.

The wooden guard posts along East Switchback Road whizzed past as Nina roared up toward the reservoir, the beam of the headlights bouncing off the white caps of each post in order. Some of the drop-offs along the winding road on this side of the mountain were fifty feet or more straight down into rugged canyons, guarded only by the wooden posts set in place by miners who had contrived the road more than a hundred years earlier, with nothing more than their mules, their backs, and their gumption. More than a few vehicles had tumbled over the side, and not been found for days. Now they were merely dark voids to Nina as she, speeding well above the posted limit, had perfect control.

Just prior to the dam, a right turn put her on the graveled Reservoir Road, which passed the reservoir to the left and a parking lot for boat trailers to the right, and a slew of camps and campers just beyond that. She wanted to stop and start asking questions but everyone seemed to be still asleep, so she decided to drive farther up the trail to the backside of the reservoir, where campers were sparse and spread out. Once at the top of the camping area she'd wait for daylight then work her way down stopping at each campsite.

The gravel road—originally a rutted trail rooted out by prospectors and miners—turned right and continued winding around the mountain and deeper into the forest. The Ford shifted into low gear when she made the turn and slowly pulled upward.

For ten minutes, she bounced along the furrowed road, constantly banging her head on a headliner until, at last, she eased the car around a small clump of fir trees to semi-hide it from casual observers, just in case Palmer was one of those observers. This would be her home for the next hour or so, until the sun came up fully. She watched slow moving gray clouds to the north, with small swelling thunderclouds starting to form well north of the mountains. But the south was amazingly clear. A bright moon was turning the vast valley below the rim into a serene, blue-gray picture postcard. Good versus evil, Nina thought, the evil pounding mountain rain—when it comes—driving out the good tranquility of the valley.

29

Sometime before daybreak, a noise that seemed disturbingly out of place awakened Pike. He had slept intermittently through the night listening to crickets, bullfrogs, and wind. But this wasn't any of them. It was more of an unnatural guttural rumble. He rolled to his side and scanned the area. There was a fine morning mist hanging over the lake but nothing else moved.

He crawled out of his sleeping bag and rekindled the fire to displace the cool, damp air, set his teapot on the flames, and laid back down to wait for the water to heat. Tea would be good for an early morning start. Again something stirred, this time with a low growl. Pike peered up and through the distortion of the rising heat of his campfire. And there, standing in the mist of the lake, was a darkened silhouette of a coyote. Pike's eyes focused, but his mind did not want to concede that the coyote stood big and tall, and up on his hind legs. Pike recalled a saying from his childhood: *Coyote is a trickster. Coyote waits in the dark to frighten. But when Coyote stands, he is pure evil.*

Pike blinked, refocused, and saw not a coyote, but an Indian standing only a few feet in front of him. The

Indian was much larger than he was and wore a cape-like coyote skin over his head and back. A yucca leaf hung between his legs and white and black streaks of paint covered his face.

"*Yee naadlooshii*," Pike whispered, "a skinwalker." Palmer had succeeded, as the old woman feared he might.

Faster than Pike could flinch, the Indian closed the gap between them, and stood directly in front of him. "Ta-ay, my woman," the Indian said and with one hand, he grabbed Pike by the throat, picked him up, and flung him into the fire. Pike rolled onto the dirt to put out the flames erupting on his shirt.

The Indian raised his foot and stomped, but Pike spun and the foot slammed into the side of his head, instead of full on. Pike stumbled forward but managed to turn and lurch at the Indian. He was nothing more than an irritant, an insignificant pest to be swatted away, and was slammed into the Corvette. He hit, rolled over the hood and staggered to his feet. He drew his knife but the Indian was on top of him in a blink, shoved the knife sideways and Pike's wrist popped then snapped as his hand was jammed rearward. The knife tumbled free. A massive fist smashed into Pike's face, sending him stumbling onto the Corvette again. When Pike regained his balance, the Indian had the knife and thrust it forward. It glanced off Pike's leather belt and penetrated the right side of his abdomen. The Indian withdrew the blade and held it at Pike's throat, stared into his eyes for a moment. Pike stared back showing no fear. *Life is often the award of bravery*. Pike stood proud and simply asked, "Why?"

144

"My woman," the Indian said and turned away. He moved to the back of the Corvette and punctured both rear tires then tossed the knife at Pike's feet. He studied Pike for a moment. "My Woman," he repeated and swiftly disappeared back into the mist of the lake.

"*Clizyati*," Pike called after the Indian. "You *are* pure evil. You leave me here to bleed to death."

Blood oozed from Pike's side and from the slit around the exposed bone at his wrist, but the agonizing pain did not stop him from pulling himself into the car, flipping the radio on, and keying the mike.

30

Nina was about to doze off when the radio crackled to life. "This is Pike," it said through enormous static, and she was about to raise hell with him when, "I need help . . . at Zuni Lake below Shadow Mountain," the words came over the speaker in spurts, static, and distress, "been attacked by a wild frigging Indian that could have been a . . . um . . . and the son of a bitch stabbed me . . . pretty bad . . . I . . . can anyone read me? Anyone . . ."

Once again there was brief silence, then more static, "Pike, this is Naize, I'm more than an hour from Shadow Mountain, but I'll try to get you help—" the radio became all static.

"What the hell was Pike doing out there this early?" Nina asked herself.

"Pike, Naize, this is Troy," the radio came back to life. Troy sounded tinny and far away. "I'm on the ground at the Rim airport."

Nina put her ear directly on the speaker. "I'm not at the airport yet, but I'm on my way, ETA below Shadow Mountain is forty minutes, over."

It took Nina a second to realize exactly how close she was to Zuni Wells. If Troy hadn't repeated the name she might not have realized it. She picked up her mike, "Troy . . . Pike, I'm between you and the reservoir, I can be there in fifteen, twenty minutes tops if I cut cross country and take the hiking trail down the back side of the mountain to FR 43, out." She did not wait for a response.

The sun was just peaking over the mountain behind her as the Ford shimmied and rattled with each rut and rock it hit along what Nina thought was a trail. She could make out trees and boulders just fine but everything else was a dark hodgepodge of smaller vegetation that she plowed through as she barreled over ridges and washes, headed straight toward Fire Road 43. At the backside of the mountain, she hit a narrow trail that dipped through a thicket of palo verde trees into a dry wash then up a long grade as it came out of the wash. The Ford downshifted and whined as it slipped and grabbed in lurches up the sandy grade of the almost impossible trail until it cleared the berm of the relatively flat FR 43. She turned right but, full of furrows, holes, and old water channels, the road was in no better shape than no road at all, but she pushed the Ford on and was glad it still had some guts.

At the top of a high ridge the road abruptly turned right and Nina stopped. To her left, down the seemingly impossible grade of the ridge and a mile south, a nine-hundred-foot monolithic rock pointed to a clear sky. To the north, Shadow Mountain, with a backdrop of ominous clouds, gave off a brilliant golden hue as the sun rose from the east, and between the two, just off the access road at Zuni Wells, Pike's red and white Corvette gleamed in the new day sunlight. Nina understood why he had picked that spot. It offered a panoramic view of the mountain, the valley, and the lake, and gave him easy access to all three.

She pulled her seatbelt as tight as possible, turned left off the fire road and pushed the accelerator pedal to the floor. The car instantly jumped to thirty, and was doing forty when it hit the downward incline. It bounced and dug its own swath through the tough vegetation, but it did not slow and was roaring past sixty when it hit a small gully at the bottom. The nose dug in, bounced out, and shot up the other side, then slammed into the ground and bounced again, but kept moving.

As Nina approached the access road south of the lake, the car hit the embankment leading up to the road at an angle and flew into the air; its left side came down first, hit the road and rebounded. Nina let out a long, audible, "ride 'em cowgirl" as the right side hit the road and tucked under. The patrol car rolled once, stripping off light harness, antennas, and side mirrors. It came to rest on its wheels, facing the mountain and Pike.

She quickly restarted the stalled engine, and drove straight to Pike.

Pike was leaning against the flattened tire of his car holding his blood-covered side, but still, with eyes wide, jaw hanging open, he managed a smile as he surveyed the Ford.

"Took a shortcut," Nina said and kicked the car door open.

She used her first-aid kit, stabilized Pike's bleeding, and had him comfortable by the time the Troy

148

landed the sturdy Waco on the dirt access road and taxied up close to the Corvette.

They wasted no time securing Pike in the open cockpit, and Troy was off to the Upland airport where an ambulance would be waiting.

Since the airplane was only a two-seater, Nina had to stay behind. She took a few minutes to look for clues, but the Indian had used the lake coming and going leaving no trail as to which way he'd gone.

She checked out Pike's Corvette. It had one spare and two flats. Upland's police force had only five patrol cars. Two were down for maintenance and one was assigned to Joe and Duke for driving patrols. That left Troy's and hers. She just needed to baby hers back to the airport and borrow Troy's for a few days. She cleaned the glass from the seat then carefully and slowly drove home, her head craning low and forward.

31

Holly waited, frightened and wide awake, cramped beneath the driftwood until the sun was bright and warm. Frightened not only of the Indian but also terrified of snakes, bugs, leeches, or some other creepy crawly slimy creature that might slither into her nest. She couldn't sleep if she wanted to.

Finally, she decided the Indian had not looked very carefully or very long because he had not once walked past her. Maybe he'd given up, maybe he'd concluded that she had drowned, but the one thing that was certain in her mind was that she wanted to be long gone while it was daylight, just in case.

Slowly and quietly, as if she might disturb him, she hobbled away from the river and into the forest, constantly looking back over her shoulder, but moving as quickly as she could. She had no idea where she was, though she was sure that the Indian had hauled her up one of the two rivers that converged at the reservoir, and if she simply followed the flow of the river it would eventually take her there. But that would take her back past the cave, and that's where he would be looking. She wasn't willing to take the chance of running headlong into him, so she turned away from the river figuring she would then double back later.

But as the sun got brighter, as the hills became taller, the valleys deeper, the woods thicker she realized that she was hopelessly lost. She now had no idea which way to go to find the river she'd left only a few hours earlier, and when she could take the heat no longer, she collapsed beneath a tree.

"Tex is not here," she told herself. "Troy isn't here either." And whatever happened from here on out, she would be on her own. If she was to survive, she realized, it would have to be on her own account.

She needed to determine a way to the river and to stop wandering aimlessly, but first things first. She needed to take care of the wound on her leg to prevent gangrene or worse. She'd heard of gangrene, wasn't sure what it was, only that they would have to cut her leg off if she got it. She examined the wound as best she could and was relieved that it didn't look infected. She removed her shirt and after several attempts managed to rip two strips from the seam at the bottom. One she folded into a pad and placed it on the wound. The other, she tied around her leg to secure the pad. The overall bandage looked good to her, and she smiled at her accomplishment. "You're doing better, girl," she told herself, and felt better about it. The wound would heal, she was now sure, and would be the least of her worries if she did not find a way out of the wilderness.

32

Pike awoke to the sound of the local television newscast predicting a massive thunderstorm coming in from the north. The television wasn't loud but he could clearly hear talk about anvil clouds, microburst, hail, and flash floods. He took in the sterile room in a glance. The fact that he was in a hospital did not come as a surprise. He remembered Nina taking care of him at the lake, the plane ride with Troy, the ride in the ambulance, and the gurney rushing into the emergency room, but little after that until he heard the television.

He tried to move his right hand to adjust his bed but his hand was useless, a cast encased it from elbow to fingertips. He fumbled for the bed control with his left hand, found it, and awkwardly raised himself to a sitting position.

Nina was asleep in a chair next to his bed.

"Hey," Pike squeaked. A dull ache consumed his entire body, but it wasn't as painful as it could have been thanks to modern drugs.

"You finally awake?" Nina asked as she stirred and stretched.

"Me? You're the one snoring.

"I don't snore."

"Uh huh," Pike said. "How long have I been here?"

"All night and most of the day."

"Did you find that crazy ass Indian?"

"Not a trace."

"And Holly?"

"Nope, we're at a dead end. I drove my wrecked cruiser around town all morning asking questions. I don't think it did any good, but it kept me busy and gave the folks something to laugh at."

"You drove that wreck home?" Pike wanted to laugh when he remembered the banged-up cruiser, but sharp pain restricted him to a huffy giggle.

"How else was I getting back? That heap of yours had two flat tires. Whoever stabbed you also got your car."

"I'll kick that painted freak's ass."

"Sure, you couldn't kick my ass right now. Let somebody else handle it."

"In that case, maybe you should be out there looking for him for me, instead of lounging around here, watching TV."

"I'm not lounging around."

"You're worried about me then?" Pike smiled.

"I'm making sure you don't do something stupid, like trying to walk out of here."

"Yeah, right," Pike said and fluttered his eyebrows. "You love me and you know it."

"Don't flatter yourself, rookie."

Pike managed another smile, but his animation also aggravated the pain. "How bad am I?" He tried to suppress a cough.

"Sadly, you'll live," Nina said. "The blade was deflected by your belt and probably saved your life. But still, you were extremely lucky that you didn't bleed to death."

"Yeah, you are my hero," Pike said. His eyes locked on hers.

"Don't get all emotional. I was only doing my job."

"Bullshit," Pike said. "You risked life and limb to come for me. Not to mention your cruiser."

"The car was a piece of crap anyway," Nina said and laughed. "And I had to look after my rookie, right?"

"Right," Pike agreed, but he wanted to believe there was more to it. He then held up his cast-covered arm to change his teary mood, "And then there's this, he snapped it like a toothpick."

"Would *he* be Palmer?" Nina asked.

"He was made up in time-honored Indian face paint and covered with a coyote skin for a while," Pike answered, "like a skinwalker, so it was hard to tell who it was."

"Like a what?"

"It has to do with Navajo witchery. It was the first thing I thought of when I saw him."

"Palmer?" Nina asked again.

"It could have been Palmer. Remember what the old Navajo woman said about him trying witchcraft. Well, from what I saw at the burial grounds, he was actually trying to perform some kind of Navajo Witchery

Way ceremony. He could have succeeded and conjured up a spirit to take over his body, to become a skinwalker. And, even though the Indian who attacked me was big and strong and moved on me so fast I couldn't react, he resembled Palmer somewhat."

"Big and strong and fast like a witch?" Nina said and laughed.

"It's not the witch, not exactly," Pike laughed with her, "it's the skinwalker."

"Uh huh," Nina giggled.

"A skinwalker," Pike said trying to sound serious, "is a spirit called upon to harass someone. He walks in another's skin, hence the name. But first he takes on the form of a nearby animal like a fox or wolf or even an owl, you know, something menacing like that. In that form his purpose is more to frighten or haunt than to harm. He appears outside someone's window and peeks in or bangs on the glass, or knocks on the walls of the house, or creeps around on the roof. If he gets bolder, he may even break into the house and try to frighten anyone inside."

Nina rolled her eyes but said nothing.

"But," Pike continued, "when a spirit is called upon to do malicious things, and the influence of the Witchery Way performance is outstanding, he usually takes on the form of a coyote, and when he rears up, you know, stands up like a man, his purpose is to do evil. At that point, he can take on the form of the person performing the witchcraft, and then he can distort that form to suite his own needs whatever that may be, but it's usually in the form of the spirit's former self."

"Uh huh," Nina said again, this time laughing. She stood, walked to the window, and looked out.

"He can't hang around long in that form though," Pike continued, knowing he was losing her interest. "But he can be summoned again and again from most anywhere on a reservation or around Indian sacred grounds where he originated. And, in that form, he can only be destroyed by an act of God, and only the witch—the one who performs the ceremony—can be killed, which is then supposed to kill the skinwalker."

"Supposed to?"

"Sometimes, if the spirit is strong enough, he can come back on his own."

"Navajo witches and ghosts. You're full of shit," Nina said chuckling.

"They're not ghosts." Pike laughed with her.

"Okay, witches then. You're still full of shit."

"They're not witches as white people know them—"

"Do I look white to you?" Nina turned and did her best Oda Mae impression from the movie *Ghost.*

Pike laughed heartily then wished he hadn't as the pain reminded him where he was. "Okay, okay, they're not witches as *non-Indians* know them. How's that?"

"Much better, Kemosabe."

"Point taken, but what I mean is that the Navajo witch looks like any other person. They don't have pointed hats, big ugly warts, ride on a broom, or twitch their cute little noses to cast a spell."

"So you, Pike Tso, could be a witch?"

"I could be, but I'm not. However, if Palmer tried hard enough, if he had the knowledge and faith that it takes, he could be."

"So it has something to do with Navajo mythology?" Nina asked.

"There's a basis for all mythology," Pike continued. "If something's misunderstood then it's labeled mythical. Just like the belief in a deity, for instance. If you have no faith, no understanding, no conviction then you'd probably call Him a myth, and many people do. But most people have the faith, and no matter how absurd you might think it is, you'd never convince them that He's a myth."

"I don't always show it or live it, but I definitely believe in God."

"Right!"

"But I've never heard of skin crawlers, yuck." Nina shivered.

"They're skin *walkers*, not crawlers." Pike laughed at her. "And I'm not surprised you've never heard of them because Navajo people normally only tell of their encounters to other Navajos, and any Navajo practicing such a ritual is considered evil because the intent is to frighten or do great harm to someone else."

"So what do the more rational Navajos believe?"

"Hmmm." Pike frowned. "They believe that if the person who performs the Witchery Way believes hard enough, has enough faith, that he himself will become detached from reality and see himself as the spirit. Like a split personality or something."

"A psychopath or schizophrenic or psychotic," Nina suggested.

"All of the above, I guess," Pike said. "And you can add multiple personality and delusions too. Non-believers can come up with all kinds of names for it."

"Why not just kidnap her? Why go to all the trouble of goblins and witches?"

"That's the whole point. Some people don't have the balls to do their dirty deeds for themselves so they call upon a spirit to do it for them."

"So Palmer wanted Holly for his own gratification but he didn't have the *nerve* to do it himself so instead of becoming a witch, why wouldn't he simply hire someone to do it for him? An accomplice you might say."

"Hire him with what?"

"That's what the ransom is for, Rookie."

"That's another possibility," Pike said, frowning.

"From the beginning I've said he had a partner."

"Makes sense," Pike agreed and tried to shrug his shoulders. "But I like my theory better."

"You would. But in any case why would he attack you?"

"A witch will call upon a skinwalker to attack and kill anyone he perceives as a threat to him or what he considers his. Palmer probably knew I was following him looking for Holly. And when he attacked me he kept referring to her as *his woman*. So if we find him, we'll find her." Pike slid his feet sideways as if he was getting out of bed.

"You're still full of shit, newbie," Nina said. "And you aren't going anywhere." She pushed the bedside nurse's call button.

158

After a couple of minutes, instead of a nurse, Doctor Miller appeared.

"Good evening, father," Nina said.

"What?" Pike fell back into bed. "Your father is a doctor?"

"Not just a doctor," Nina said with a big grin, "but he's *your* doctor."

Doctor Miller was round and jovial, the antithesis of Nina. He smiled, big and proud. "How are you doing, Mister Tso?"

"I need to get out of here," Pike said.

"He needs morphine, or something," Nina said, "to put him out of his misery."

"I don't need morphine or something," Pike said. "I need out of here."

"He's babbling," Nina said to her father. "He's been babbling about witches and crap since he woke up, ignore him and give him something."

"Witches, huh? Well, I've got a potion right here that'll do the trick." Doctor Miller held up a hypodermic. "And I have enough to put both of you out of *my* misery—" he looked at his daughter and smiled "—if you don't clear out of here and let my patient rest."

33

Because of his unexplainable disgust of horses, Justman walked the last two miles to the top of Squaw Butte. He'd driven the county truck to the base of the butte as far as it would go, then camouflaged it as best he could beneath two scrubby overhanging palo verde trees before setting out on foot. Then, step by miserable step, carrying a backpack full of ham sandwiches and bottled water for his long journey, he'd slogged up the steep grades, around studded piñon, jumping cholla, and prickly pear to get to the top.

At the top of the butte, Justman cautiously remained concealed in the underbrush. In his ransom note, he had specifically said no one was to be on or near the butte during the drop, but he had no way of knowing for sure if he was indeed alone. Troy could have already had the place staked out, which is something he would have done if the situation were reversed. You never know about cops these days, Justman thought and laughed at himself.

He sat on the bare dirt, washed down a sandwich with a bottle of water, and waited until nothing stirred but the wind and a lone buzzard circling in the hazy distance. He waited until absolutely sure he was alone. And then he carefully circled the butte and found the backpack hanging from the branches of a short piñon tree. The backpack was much smaller and lighter than he had envisioned, but he didn't bother to look inside, not even for his own amusement, because he knew the money would be there. He doubted Troy would take any foolish chances with his beautiful wife's life. And Troy's wife was without doubt beautiful, Justman reminded himself. In fact, he had thought about her almost nonstop since she was abducted. He had convinced himself that Red Hawk would soon have her hogtied somewhere within the confines of an ancient Indian stronghold, introducing her to his new beginning. The crazy, fucking Indian would have her naked, Justman imagined, tied spread-eagle to a chair or a bed or something similar, doing God knows what to her. That thought was starting to bother him immensely, and arouse him beyond even his own belief. She was too beautiful to waste on the grubby, psycho.

He quickly slung the small backpack over the one he was already carrying and, instead of heading for his truck, instead of taking the money to Silverwood to be laundered, instead of completing his beautiful plan, he began the four-mile trudge down the back side of Squaw Butte, halfway up Shadow Mountain, and deep into its arcane forest. Because Red Hawk had wasted an enormous amount of time in town and would be on foot dragging Holly with him, Justman was sure that if he hustled he had a good chance of beating the Indian to the stronghold. He hustled.

34

Troy now flew slow lazy S's, crisscrossing between the reservoir, Squaw Butte, and Shadow Mountain. He had left the hospital as soon as Doctor Miller informed him that Pike was going to be all right, gone home, showered, and gotten a relatively good night's sleep. Had breakfast with Jesse and Blonde, packed a small backpack with supplies—including flashlight, beef sandwiches, and a first-aid kit—found a canteen and a fifty-foot coil of rope , and was back at the airport at daylight. He had once again promised Beth McDonald that he would call her soon and took off at tree level.

As the plane made wide, meandering turns, he scrutinized the ground and underbrush just a few feet below him, looking for any sign of anyone doing anything out of the ordinary, all the while keeping an eye on the transceiver. He tried to make sense of what had happened as the plane skimmed along the treetops. Everyone seemed sure that Red Hawk, now Palmer, was the kidnapper, holding Holly captive at the reservoir or Zuni Wells or somewhere in between. And Pike had said that the Indian who attacked him resembled Palmer and had referred to someone as his woman. If he was talking about Holly then it certainly made sense that Palmer was in the forest, within the triangle formed by Zuni Wells, Upland Reservoir, and Shadow Mountain. But so much more did not make sense to Troy. Like, why would Palmer abduct Holly, demand a ransom, and then declare her his woman? And why dress up like some crazed Indian to attack Pike? Was the idea to frighten him? Is that what he did to Holly, frighten her by dressing up like a Halloween Indian? But Troy wasn't sure Palmer had the mental capacity to engineer and execute such a plan, not for money anyway. Unless of course he had an accomplice, as Nina believed.

The only other explanation would be pure chance, pure circumstance. Someone, an Indian—Palmer even—happened to be walking along and there was Holly riding her horse alone, and he decided to waylay her, right then and there without prudence. But why abduct her? If it was the crime of impulsive passion, a crime of opportunity for the sole purpose of gratification, then there would be no reason for a ransom note, unless the ransom was an afterthought or perpetuated by someone else, an accomplice or partner, or someone taking advantage of a convenient situation. It would have to be someone who needed money badly, someone who looked like an Indian and had great knowledge of Indians and their ways. Someone like Pike or Naize or Justman, maybe. But Pike would not have stabbed himself, and Naize could not have known that Troy had a substantial bank account, and Justman, well, he was a good cop and Troy had known him for years.

Something to think about, Troy told himself, but not now. All of that could be considered later. Right now it didn't matter who had taken Holly and for what reason, Troy's quest was to find her. She had to be out there somewhere within the triangle he had drawn on his chart. She had to be.

At the base of Squaw Butte, the side farthest from Shadow Mountain, he spotted a sheriff's pickup truck, semi-hidden beneath two trees. Troy made a quick circle around the truck. It appeared abandoned. Maybe it had been there for weeks or months and he'd overlooked it before. He could only hope that Justman or Naize wasn't out there interfering to the point of putting Holly in danger.

Then, on a side road that snaked below Shadow Mountain, two deputies on horseback were slowly making their way up the mountain. Troy circled them and they waved. More people to put Holly in jeopardy; he wished they had all stayed away for a little longer. He tried to contact them with his handheld radio, but static from the pending storm and prop noise prevented any possible communications.

Troy moved on, up the mountain in the direction the deputies were traveling, and, on a sparse ridge several miles north and well up the side of Shadow Mountain, the red light on his small transceiver began to blink. He made a sharp three-hundred-sixty degree circle and got a glimpse of a lone person, burdened with two backpacks, dodging through the trees at a hasty pace.

***

When Justman realized that Troy was tracking him, he crawled under a pile of brush, out of sight, and transferred the money from Troy's backpack into his own while the plane circled above him. He turned the backpack inside-out and found the transmitter. He cursed himself for being so careless as he crushed it into tiny pieces between two rocks. Then, darting from tree to tree, he moved on up the mountain.

***

When the blinking suddenly stopped, Troy hurriedly marked the spot on his chart, plotting a straight line in the direction the person had been moving in hopes of pinpointing a destination, but could find nothing on the chart that made sense to him, just wilderness.

Troy continued to circle looking for a place to land; there was nothing but miniscule clearings among the trees and the river. He wanted to be on the ground now. The guy down there had his money and would no doubt lead him to Holly. But it wouldn't do anyone any good if he killed himself trying to set down on the river or between large and thick trees. If he had a parachute, he told himself, he'd jump on the spot where the transmitter had died, and let the plane fly on, on its own, until it ran out of fuel.

Instead, he turned south and headed toward Zuni Wells, the closest place he could think of to land.

***

Holly had tramped from one shady spot to another. That morning the sun had risen behind a mass of clouds and the dawn was cool. But now, beyond the rim of the clouds the sun was glaringly bright and hot. She looked for dense foliage for protection, and struggled to stay on her feet. She considered giving up, simply lying down and going to sleep, but then she suddenly became aware of a loud, ear-piercing noise. It had been there for some time, droning on in the background, but she had paid little attention. It was some distance away, but coming straight toward her, growing louder by the second. She waited, holding her breath in disbelief. It was an airplane. Were they looking for her, or were they there for some other reason? It didn't matter to her as long as they were coming. When she saw the plane, it was so low over the trees that its wheels were clipping the tallest ones and its propeller was disrupting everything in its path. And it was canary-yellow with two sets of wings, one on top of the other. "It's Troy's plane!" She cried out and couldn't control the burst of tears as she jumped up and down waving her arms, screaming at the top of her lungs, "down here, down here." She ran to find a clear area, continually waving her arms and screaming, but the tree foliage was everywhere. The plane circled in a tight loop then flew away in the direction from which it had come. "I'm over here! I'm over here! Why can't you see me?" she shrieked as it disappeared over the trees. Tripping and stumbling, she ran headlong after it until the roar of the engine was again only an echo in her ears. It disappeared as quickly as it had appeared.

Deflated and angry with herself for not being visible, she stumbled to a large boulder at the edge of an outcropping of rocks, fell beside it, put her face in her hands and cried. She should have known Troy would be out here. She should have known.

***

At Zuni Wells, Troy set the plane down in almost the same tracks he'd created earlier, and taxied up close to Pike's abandoned Corvette. It was the nearest landing spot he could find.

Troy could see the swath of dirt and vegetation Nina had created coming down from the reservoir and across the various washes to get to the lake. The drive had to have been exciting to say the least, Troy mused, and figured that following her path to the base of the incline she came down, then finding a way around the mountain to the river would be a much easier walk than the route he had planned for himself. He had decided to take the mountain straight on, up and through Siphon Draw. It would be a hard climb, but would cut several hours off his journey. His goal was to reach the spot where he had picked up the radio signal as soon as possible.

Troy pulled the backpack from the front seat of the airplane, adjusted the straps to fit, placed it and a canteen of water over his shoulders, and slung the fifty-foot coil of rope over the canteen strap. He let the equipment bounce on his hip as he put the plane, and Pike's Corvette, behind him.

35

Holly cried only for a little while, just long enough to quit feeling sorry for herself. Then she forced herself up and onward, mostly in the direction the plane had flown. She staggered down one ridge and up another until she stopped at the bottom of a steep, upward slopping scrubby box canyon.

The climb looked possible even for her, as tired and beat up as she was, so she started upward with thoughts of higher ground so Troy could see her when he returned. And the thought of finding a water pool among the crevasses above her buoyed her enthusiasm, such as it was. However, as the rocky cliffs closed in and the ascent became impossibly hard for her, out of breath and out of energy, she was about to turn back when the canyon opened up. At this point it was mostly void of vegetation, and full of cave-like hollows that covered the rocky walls like the holes of a giant sponge. Holly wandered into the canyon and ambled from one hollow to the next hoping that at least one would contain water, even if it was just a mud hole. Instead of water, she found an abundance of drawings of stars, moons, suns, checkerboard squares, birds, bighorn sheep, snakes, mountain lions, wolves, scorpions, lizards, and people, all scratched into the rocks centuries ago. She had heard about places like this and was amazed that hunters and prospector had respected this one's existence all these years by not defacing any of the depictions.

A waning shaft of sunlight caught her eye as it hit upon one illustration, and she recoiled backward then froze in place. Scratched in the middle of a rock, a creature, part human and part coyote with a zigzag face and burning, piercing eyes, glared at her. It was the unmistakable image of the Indian that had abducted her. The depiction showed him in the middle of various animals and natives that appeared to be running from him. Holly stood motionless until it faded into darkness, and the canyon quickly became a hodgepodge of pitch-black voids as the sun mercifully fell behind the mountain.

She reversed course and, stumbling with every step, she clambered back down the direction she had come.

Once out of the canyon and back where she had started, she lay beside a small boulder beneath several trees and refused to close her eyes. She laid awake most of the night, shivering and cold, and thought about dying.

36

Although overweigh and out of shape, Justman had kept a solid, respectable pace up the rugged terrain. In his entire life, nothing had inspired him to such a grueling feat as the thought of what the Indian might do to Holly if he did not get there first. It didn't help that Troy was constantly flying back and forth, so close above the trees that he'd felt the prop wash, making him deviate several times from his intended path. However, drenched in sweat and gasping for breath, he'd kept the grueling pace for three solid hours until, almost ready to crumble under his own weight, he'd found the decaying wooden hut backed up against one of many walls of rock that encompassed the area that Red Hawk had described as Cochise's stronghold. The hut, well hidden beneath thick overhanging branches of ponderosas, was also just as the Indian had described it.

Relieved that there was no sign of Red Hawk, Justman now eased his way through the flimsy door. He would hole up and take a much deserved break while he waited for Red Hawk and Holly. A shaky wooden table with two equally wobbly chairs dominated the center of the room, an empty, dust and cobweb-covered shelf hung on one wall, and a collapsed rock fireplace held the back wall in place. The furniture and fireplace, such as they were, were obviously brought in well after Cochise's reign.

Already amused at the thought of this being Red Hawk's dream house, when Justman dumped the contents of the backpack and the ten packets of hundred dollar bills tumbled onto the dusty tabletop, he giggled like a school kid. All the effort he had expended stumbling through the woods for most of the day was suddenly worth it.

And he continued to giggle at the thought of Troy's plane droning overhead because he knew that Troy could not see the stronghold through the dense trees and walls of rock no matter how low he flew, and that he was safe inside.

Justman built a small fire in the crumbling fireplace for light and heat in case he had to spend the night there. Then he casually sat down to eat another sandwich, and contemplate his brilliance. Of course Justman had a distasteful sense about what he was doing because he didn't consider himself a bad person, not really. He still had the traditional Indian values toward others that Jay Uqualla had bestowed on him, and he was a good cop even if only by his own estimation. But as soon as he realized the daft Indian had carried out the kidnapping, he knew riches were within his grasp. And the possibility of being with Holly for just one night was more than he could resist—another opportunity presenting itself that he could not pass up. But as soon as this ordeal was over, he had no doubt that he'd go back to being a good cop, out of debt, with money in the bank.

37

"You know I should've played that game against you instead of allowing Kid to do it," J.C. said to Hog. They sat at the bar, J.C. twisting the gold and diamond ring he wore on his pinky finger. The solid silver band had a flat gold face that depicted a nine-ball. The ball was thirty-six small-cut diamonds laid side-by-side in a circle with eighteen more diamonds of the same size forming the 9. J.C. glanced in wonderment around the saloon as he spoke. He owned both ring and saloon thanks to a combination of Kid's grand pool-playing abilities, excellent nerve for a then thirteen-year-old, and some astounding luck.

"No, you did it just right," Hog said. "You were in such bad shape with the drinkin and all. I would have shucked you bad, and I would be the proud owner of that ring and the saloon. Kid held his own and look what it got you. Sure he got lucky at the end, but that's part of the game."

"I've always felt like I betrayed myself by not standing up to my principles."

"Christ, J.C., you know you don't have any principles," Hog said. "But you do have a saloon and that friggin pinky ring is still yours."

"Humph," J.C. mumbled. "Maybe I'll give the ring to you someday. You always did like it."

"Maybe we'll play for it someday. Or maybe I'll play Kid for it someday. But one thing for sure, you ain't gonna *give* it to me.

J.C. smiled but said nothing.

"Anyway," Hog continued. "You are doin the right thing playin this game against your California buddy. This one you can't slough off on Kid."

"Buddy, my ass."

"Blondie still doesn't know about the game, does she?" Dana asked as she set another glass of water in front of them, and smiled at Hog for not insisting on something stronger in front of J.C.

"Blissfully unaware," J.C. answered. "As long as she stays at Troy's house watching the baby, she'll never know."

"If she does find out, she's not going to like it," Dana said. "You guys playing pool for her. It's crazy stupid."

"Change the subject," J.C. said searching his shirt pocket for a phantom pack of cigarettes. "I don't even want to think about it."

"Well, the saloon is packed," Dana stated the obvious. "Business is good and you're living pretty well."

J.C. looked at his water glass, shoved it aside. "Christ O' Mighty, Dana," he said. "You call this living? And the reason we're so busy is, in his effort to embarrass me, old Jiffy spread the word, running up and down the street, like the moron he is, selling everyone on what a big deal the pool game is going to be. How I'm finally going to get my due because, in his estimation, Rabbit has the smoothest stroke that has ever been in the saloon, as if he doesn't remember me before I got old and decrepit."

"Rabbit's beaten everyone he's played since comin to town, and by a wide margin," Hog said. "He even beat his number one fan, Jiffy, out of a week's wages even after givin up the five-ball. He's pretty damn good. You can't deny that."

"Jiffy can't play for shit," J.C. said in his growling undertone.

"With the five-ball, he should be able to beat most players," Hog said.

Through the window, J.C. watched a chaotic swarm of people spill across the sidewalk and into the street, all headed for the saloon. "It's just like it was two years ago, he said, "when the ambulance had to maneuver through the stubborn crowd to get to the front door to haul Troy off to the hospital after Black Berry shot him."

"I remember," Hog said. "A few minutes later, the Mexican Mafia guys nearly creamed a bunch of them when they roared around the corner in their limousine to kill Black Berry, who was about to shoot you in case you've forgotten. That was a close one, as I recall. And, at the same time, in front of this same packed house, Kid put an end to my saloon-owning days. Of course I remember."

"There're all screwballs," J.C. said still looking at the crowd through the window. "It's just another bullshit pool game. Why can't these idiots just go home and leave me be?"

"You mean before Blondie finds out?" Dana asked.

J.C. just frowned at her.

"They don't see it as bullshit," Hog said. "They're starved for excitement around here and you're the closest thing to a celebrity they have, everyone thinks so."

"Celebrity, my ass. It's a pathetic bunch who thinks I'm something I'm not. Maybe they should all go home and sleep it off."

"It's good for business." Dana reminded him again.

"Whatever," J.C. said and looked at his watch, "it is getting late; I guess it's time to give them what they want so they'll have something stimulating to talk about at work tomorrow." He pushed himself from the bar and rambled toward the back room where the 1890 Brunswick pool table had been sitting for well over a hundred years. He wandered past dining tables and booths getting high-fives, pats on the back, and "good lucks" from most of the patrons.

Inside the pool table room, Rabbit sat high on a spectator's chair with his cue standing upright between his legs. "'Bout fucking time," he said. "I was beginning to think that maybe you were going to be chicken shit and bail on me."

"You mean you were hoping," J.C. said as he surveyed the pool table. The balls were tightly racked, in perfect order, but the table itself had not been re-felted since Kid's game two years earlier. The now threadbare cloth, however, with its ruts, dings, and nicks would be to his advantage since he was used to it. Slowly and carefully, he screwed the shaft onto the butt of his rebuilt Rambow, scuffed chalked onto the tip, and blew the residue from it.

"Christ O' Mighty," J.C. said. "Let's do this."

Hog blocked the doorway from the distraction of onlookers simply by standing in it.

38

Justman did not have to wait long. He had sat down on one flimsy chair and propped his feet up on the other for a much-needed rest, and was about to open his second soggy sandwich when the door burst open. The top leather hinge gave way as the door slammed the thatched wall, and then hung open at an awkward slant. Justman could see only the Indian's silhouette filling the doorway as the setting sunlight streamed through the dust past him.

"Surprise!" Justman said, smiling.

The Indian said nothing.

"I really didn't think you had the balls to actually kidnap her." Justman looked past him, through the open door, letting his eyes adjust. "Where the hell is she?"

"Missing," the Indian said.

Justman's eyes now fixed on the Indian, whose voice, mannerism, and size were somehow different. "Look, you crazy fuck, I'm aware she's missing. The whole fucking town is looking—" Justman suddenly realized that it wasn't Red Hawk he was staring at, not exactly. He resembled Red Hawk, at least he did at first, but now? And he was almost naked, except for a strap that held a couple of leaves in front of him and a knife sheathed at his side. And his face was streaked black and white. Justman had not noticed that before. "What the hell are you trying to pull, you crazy bastard?" Justman let the chair slam down on all four legs and stood to get a better look. He instinctively pulled his pistol at the same time. "Who the fuck are you?"

"My woman, Ta-ay," the Indian said.

"Your woman? You fucking retard, you're frightened of your own breath. You'd have a heart attack if she just looked at you, and if you didn't, you wouldn't know what to do with her." Justman pointed the pistol at the Indian's crotch. "You either tell me where she is or I'll blow your fucking balls off. Then you won't need her. Comprende?"

"Ta-ay, my woman." The Indian's fist came from nowhere and so fast that it caught Justman in the side of his head before he could react, before he could pull the trigger, and he went sprawling half unconscious to the floor. But adrenaline and reflex pulled him around and he rolled to his knees, leveled the pistol and fired.

In one flawless blur the Indian crossed the room, his snake-handled knife thrust forward.

Justman pulled the trigger again as the knife passed through his throat. Blood spewed as he looked on in horror, then fell backward onto the floor.

The Indian watched the blood gurgle until it merely dribbled. Then, with ease, he moved to the table and sat down. He pulled the now blood-covered sandwich to him and began to eat. The blood of the white-eyes would be good.

178

39

Daylight was fading quickly so Troy hurriedly tracked as straight a course as possible, keeping the lake behind him, always mindful that whoever stabbed Pike could be watching in case he got too close. The walk was a slow, gradual two-mile incline to the base of the mountain where it was split by a natural draw called Siphon Draw—so called because of the enormous chimney-effect it had pulling the wind savagely upward. The draw led up to the more hospitable tree-studded terrain above the rampart that made up that side of the mountain, and Troy hoped to reach the top before dark. One handhold at a time, he started his ascent, and slowly advanced, walls rising steadily on both sides. The ever-darkening narrow gorge became a black, enveloping slit, where straight up, an array of bright stars were the only source of light—and now his only way out.

The relentless wind pulled up the draw, and gained strength as he climbed. It pushed hard at his back, buoying him against the hard climb, pressing him up the last few feet to the top where he stopped only long enough to survey his options. On the back side of the draw was a small ledge where he could find refuge away from the relentless push of the wind. Carefully, he slid down the embankment to the ledge. From there, if he waited until daylight, it would be an easy down hill descent.

Exhausted, he collapsed on the ledge, feet dangling over the side. He removed his gear, unzipped the backpack to retrieve one of his beef sandwiches, but immediately realized that he wasn't alone. He could hear a distinct rattle. Gradually, he turned toward the depth of the gap at the back of the ledge, straining to see into the blackness. The noise continued in a steady, rhythmic rattle. Troy spun sideways placing his backpack between him and the noise just as a six-foot rattlesnake struck the backpack then recoiled. Though slow and lethargic, it struck with force. Sure he'd stumbled upon a nest, probably one very perturbed adult and several babies, Troy moved precariously close to the edge. He didn't like his odds and was considering the possibility of jumping when the snake struck the backpack again.

And Troy tumbled into the darkness.

40

When Pike awoke the drapes were open and, though filtered and dull by high clouds, the morning sun lit up the room. Nina was again asleep, but this time on an overstuffed chair with her feet propped up on a matching ottoman. He cleared his throat, but she did not notice. He cleared it again, this time more loudly.

Nina sat straight up, as if she'd not been asleep at all.

"What are you still doing here?" Pike asked.

"Keeping an eye on you."

"You're worried about me?" Pike smiled broadly.

"You're our rookie, the only newbie we've had since I joined the force, and Troy told me to watch over you. I think he feels a little responsible for your sorry butt."

"Sure," Pike said, "fault Troy if you like, but it's starting to look as though you do like me, and my beautiful butt."

"Don't get your hopes up, Injun," Nina answered with a smile.

"Where'd you get the chair?"

"The nurse and I stole it from the doctor's lounge. I think it's my father's, nice, huh?"

"Probably more comfortable than this bed."

"Wanna trade?"

"Are you kidding me? Nurse Ratchet would have a shit-fit."

"Be nice. She's taking good care of you."

"In that case, where's the coffee? I'm in desperate need of a caffeine fix."

"Ask and you shall receive," Nina said and jumped from her plush chair. "I could use a cup myself. But when I get back, I have to go. Brother J.C. started another one of his crazy pool games at the saloon last night, and the whole town showed up, again. What a mess."

"Pool game?"

"Holly's missing, you've been stabbed, Troy's running around in the mountains alone and probably lost, and the only thing this town has on its mind is J.C.'s bullshit pool game. Even Duke and Joe talk about how it's something extraordinary."

"What's it all about?"

"You've heard about his other escapades?"

"Everyone knows. He lost the saloon way back when, then won it back a couple of years ago. Playing Nine Ball, I think."

"Right, three people died, Troy was shot and the crowds were almost uncontrollable."

"Over a pool game?"

"He's our local celeb. Some say he could have been one of the top players in the country, if not the top. But all he brought us is mayhem and amusement.

"So what's *this* game all about?"

"Apparently he's playing his wife's lover or ex-lover or whatever, and the prize is her."

"No shit?"

"True story. And the winner gets to keep her. So the crazies are showing up again to watch or at least keep tabs on the game for their side bets, and I need to be on the streets when it's over."

"Are you sure I want to work for this town?"

Nina shrugged, smiled, and headed for the coffee machine two floors down.

Pike's eyes were about to close again when Nina's radio startled him. She'd left it on the stand beside his bed.

"Nina, this is Duke. Are you handy?"

Pike had been thinking about his own pool-playing abilities. He had tried it a few times at the Indian bars near the reservation, but was horrible. He simply could not figure out how to cue the cue ball in any manner to make it travel straight, let alone making any ball in any given pocket, on purpose. This lack of ability cost him many beers. And, now, the idea that he knew someone who could have ranked as a top player, better than anyone else in the country, purely amazed him.

"Nina, this is Duke."

Pike rolled sideways, managed to snag the radio by its antenna with his left hand, and hoist it to his face. "What's up, Duke?"

"Pike? Is that you? How you doing, buddy?"

"Looks like I'll survive."

"That's good news. . . . Is Nina there?"

"She went to get coffee."

"Are you two an item?" Duke asked and laughed. "She's a good girl; we all think the world of her around here."

"In my dreams," Pike answered and sighed.

Duke laughed again. "I'll come up and visit you, if I ever get relieved."

"Don't worry about that, what's up?"

"I've got some bad news, buddy. I tried to contact Troy but couldn't get through to him."

"Okay, I'm lying down," Pike said. "Let me have it."

"Justman's dead."

"Bullshit, I just saw him the other day. . . . Thomas Justman, the deputy sheriff? Are you sure?"

"Just like you, he was stabbed. But he didn't survive. He was at an old Indian stronghold on Shadow Mountain that most people don't even know exists. County Sheriff's office, a deputy named Naize actually, called, said some Hopi tribal policemen on horseback found him while looking for Holly. Naize also tried to contact Troy but couldn't get through to him either, must have his radio turned off."

"What the hell was Justman doing up there?"

"Looking for the kidnapper, I suppose. And it looks like he found the turd too. Then they fought and the wrong guy won."

"If it was the same maniac who attacked me, there was no way Justman was going to take him." Pike said. "He tries to kill me by the lake one day then climbs the mountain and kills Justman the next. What the hell? Where's the connection?"

"Don't know about any connection, but maybe you guys were getting too close to him. And Shadow Mountain, that's where Troy went."

"Shit," Pike said. "I'd sure feel better if we could contact him."

"Tell me about it."

"Has everyone else been informed?" Pike asked.

"Yeah, Naize said he also called DPS, and of course the FBI was contacted yesterday about the kidnapping. Their guys will be here today, screwing around.

"We can use their resources," Pike said.

"Way too much paperwork for what they have to offer. Anyway, Naize wants Nina to contact him when she gets a chance."

"Thanks," Pike said and immediately switched the radio to the sheriff department's frequency. "Upland Police Officer Pike Tso here, does anyone copy?"

"Hey, cousin, I copy." Deputy Naize answered almost immediately then chuckled. "I understand you cut yourself and landed in the hospital."

"Some minor thing," Pike said. "Anyway, I just got word about Justman. I'm sorry, are you all right?"

"Yeah, thanks. We're all saddened but he wasn't best friends with anyone here, they all thought he was a joke, you know, trying to be an Indian and all. But never mind that now; at least he died a hero."

"Really?"

"From the looks of things, he found Troy's ransom money in some hut up on the mountain and had transferred it into his own backpack for safe keeping before the kidnapper surprised him and killed him."

"The money was still there when they found Justman?"

"That's what I understand. Apparently the killer, not knowing that Justman had the money, took off with Troy's empty backpack since it wasn't found. But I didn't make the trip. I let the Hopi's handle the scene this time. I'm not climbing up there if I don't have to. I'll leave that shit to the *frigging* Indians."

"We're being a little racist, enit?" Pike said.

"Not when an Indian says it. It's only racist when a white man says it."

"I never did understand that twisted logic."

"Me either, but I use it. Anyway, evidently Justman's neck was severed, nearly decapitated."

"Jesus," Pike said. "Was Holly there?"

"No one knows, but they didn't find her, if that's what you're asking."

"Dumb question, I guess," Pike said. "But something about this whole thing stinks."

"If the Hopi's find anything relative, I'll get on a stupid horse, ride up there tomorrow and take a look myself. I hate horses."

"What is it with you guys and horses? Justman hated them too, but you're a real Indian, and you hate horses?" Pike asked just as Nina walked into the room. She was holding two cups of coffee.

"I am true blood forever and ever," Naize said. "But, like Justman, I never did like horses."

"When we find Holly," Nina said, "we'll have her teach you how to ride."

"Ain't gonna happen," Naize said. "In the meantime, Pike will fill you in about Justman. I have to go. Any word on Troy?"

"Negative," Nina answered.

"Is he still in the forest?"

Nina hesitated then said, "I'm not sure, he may be on his way back."

"Gotta go." Naize said abruptly and was gone.

"What was that?" Pike asked. "You know Troy's not on his way back."

"I don't like or trust Justman," Nina said, "and he's Justman's partner." She handed Pike his coffee, then rubbed her nose with her middle finger.

"Justman's dead." Pike said straight out.

"Dear God. How?"

"He was stabbed to death. He was up in the mountains looking for Holly."

"And I believed he was behind this somehow."

"Apparently not."

"Was it Palmer slash Red Hawk?"

"I believe it might be something more powerful than Palmer."

41

When Holly awoke, she had no idea where she was or which way she should go and little hope of figuring it out. The hot and bright sun was once again high above the mountain. She sat on the boulder, in the shade of trees, and listened for Troy's plane. It wasn't there, not even in the background far, far away. She could only hear the wind rustle through the trees, and the birds call as they gracefully darted from branch to branch without a care in the world, without once stumbling. The wind had shifted and become humid. She could smell the decay of the earth beneath her, the rot of things dead.

All living things die and are returned back to earth.

Dust to dust, from whence they came.

She fumbled with the bandage on her leg. It was loose and dirty so she discarded it. The gash on her thigh was red, swollen, and bleeding a little, but still didn't look terribly infected. She replaced the bandage with two more strips from the bottom of her shirt. "Why bother?" she asked herself but did it anyway.

Her lips were parched and her stomach growled. She briefly considered climbing back up into the canyon to look for water again, but the place spooked her and there was no way she wanted to see the Indian again, not even the hundred year old figure chiseled into a rock version. No way. Then she wondered if the depiction was even real or was it a figment of her imagination. Was this whole ordeal a figment of her imagination? Maybe she was simply dreaming.

"Wake up, Holly," she said as she pushed herself up and hopelessly struggled forward. "Wake up." Her mind wandered from one thing to another until it again settled on Tex. She didn't want to think of him, but wasn't able to stop herself either. Tex, she recalled, knew where the fun was—the late-night parties, and cowboy bars along the rodeo circuit, and motels where they could have a good time. He always had enough cash to do whatever he wanted and wasn't stingy with it. Though often mentally abusive in his redneck ways, she recalled, he did take her places and bought her things to keep her satisfied, little things, but things she'd been without most of her life, including many used books. Mostly romance novels, but good ones too, she recalled. She and Tex were, if not happy then certainly carefree, and had lots of joyful times together. But fun and games was all it was, she now confessed to herself. It couldn't possibly have been love, not really. Love had to be more than fun and games, or surely she would have felt some exceptional loss when she left him for Troy. In the past, she had of course blamed Tex for bringing her to Upland. The small backwoods town that had consumed her soul, robbed her of her spirit. If she had failed to do so, she would now forgive him.

She licked her parched lips but her mouth was too dry to do any good, and she wished she had something to drink, thought about collapsing, but meandered onward. Why had she left the river? All that water and she had no idea which way it was.

Where was the airplane?

Troy, unlike Tex, was as solid as a rock, he loved her beyond doubt and reason, and she knew it. If only she'd grown up fast enough to realize that when she had the chance, maybe she would not be in the predicament she was in now. She should have known all along that Troy would risk everything, "life and limb" as they say, to come to her aid. She looked deep into a gorge at her left then gazed up into the swaying trees on the mountain at her right. He was out there somewhere looking for her. She could feel it. But hopelessness once again set in because she also realized that he had no way of knowing where she was.

All living things die and are returned back to earth.

Dust to dust, from whence they came.

She couldn't get that out of her mind "All living things must die," she mumbled. She had been wandering in circles, she was now certain, everything looked familiar, and she wondered how she could possibly be walking in a circle. The sun was always there, to her left or was it on her right? She would have to rest. Her mind was wandering and she couldn't think straight. She needed to close her eyes for a while and consider what she was doing. She needed sleep. She needed water. Her mind drifted and she wished she was at home with Troy and Jesse, where she belonged. But that was now impossible, beyond her grasp. She had blamed Troy for her misery. But that was wrong too, and she now understood it. Troy had given her everything. "God," she said, now calling on a deity she had no use for in the past. "If you are there, it's Troy and my son that I love."

Maybe she was getting soft, preparing herself for the inevitable, starting to believe she would not survive, knowing the end was near, and she was trying to make amends. If that's the case, she decided, she would also forgive her father and mother and grandfather for any indiscretions they might have had, for the turmoil they caused in her youth.

She wanted—no needed—to forgive everyone before she died.

All living things die and are returned back to earth.

Dust to dust, from whence they came.

The sun blazed through the clouds. Holly licked at her dry lips again, with her dry tongue. Her mind digressed back to her childhood, to the wonderland of Alice, a story her mother had first read to her when she was a youngster, then she'd read herself many times afterwards. Alice only had to think of something to make it appear. When Alice rushed off looking for the White Rabbit's house, there it was. And, as if thinking about the story and the White Rabbit's house made it so, just like Alice, when Holly looked up, there it was. She had not seen it before. Where had it been? She looked around for the White Rabbit, for an explanation. She staggered up the dusty trail and, there, among the pine and spruce and underbrush stood the little house. It was square, without windows, with a metal roof and large rusty door.

Holly walked to the door. An enormous padlock hooked through an even larger clasp barred her entrance. She was not surprised, for on the other side, she knew, there would be *the loveliest garden you ever saw.* But she needed a key, and she turned to look for the three-legged, glass-topped table, and the golden key. When she couldn't find it, tears filled her eyes, ran down her cheeks, and streaked her dirty face. She walked to the shady side of the White Rabbit's house and curled up, away from the sun, on the hot, dry dirt. "Dust to dust," she said and cried herself to sleep, waiting for the White Rabbit and the tears to shrink her so she could creep beneath the door, to the *beds of bright flowers and those cool fountains* that lay on the other side. Cool fountains with water, she thought. If only she had water.

"All living things must die . . ."

42

Troy came to in a sweat, lying at the bottom of a small canyon. The sun was blasting through an abundance of clouds, scorching the already hot earth and rocks around him. His head throbbed with a dull pain, his arms and legs tingled with numbness. He examined himself. Nothing appeared broken or mangled and, though painful, no lacerations or contusions seemed life threatening.

With every muscle and joint in pain, he shuffled around the canyon floor and found his canteen, rope, and backpack containing only one sandwich, a couple of energy bars, but no radio. He looked up the steep wall of stone and figured the rest of the contents of his backpack and the radio were high above him on the ledge, with the snake. He had no desire to retrieve any of it, not that the radio worked in the mountains anyway.

The canyon was full of dark boulders and clusters of mountain grass that leaned inward with the pull of a building wind, and very few scrubby trees and sage. Hollows of various sizes and shapes lined the walls of the canyon, ancient Indian dwellings, Troy guessed. Depictions of animals and natives, etched in the rocks became more visible as sunlight stretched down into the canyon. Briefly, Troy wondered how the native people of different tribes could come and go, and still keep their history straight with only crude drawings. Or, he wondered, were they just doodlings with no significant purpose and not history at all? Art, maybe, carved in rock walls by social misfits of their time, and nothing more. In any case, the canyon obviously held some sacred meaning to the natives from so long ago. He would hold that same reverence for it.

He also found a trail of broken grasses and overturned rocks where a person or persons with scant hiking experience had recently stumbled around before backtracking out of the canyon. Troy took two long draws of water, secured his backpack, slung everything else over his shoulders and, limping, followed the recent trail out of the canyon. He appreciated the fact that he was now climbing down instead of up.

Finally out of the canyon, he staggered to a boulder in the shade of a tree and took a seat. The fall from the ledge had taken its toll, more so than he'd first thought but, still, he rested for only a few minutes to catch his breath then packed up to leave. As he slung his backpack over his shoulder, his eyes caught two strips of cloth lying in the weeds beside the boulder. He picked them up and examined then. They were discarded bandages of some kind. Although the blood had dried it still had substance and a dark ruddy hue, indicating that it was relatively fresh. He looked at the material, felt its texture, and studied its color closely. He'd seen it before.

Then he let out a low whistle and mumbled, "Son of a bitch," when he realized they were torn from Holly's riding shirt. He sat back down on the boulder—the same rock she had most likely sat on while a wound, probably hers, was being tended to. With all he had been through and as big as the wilderness was, he had stumbled onto the trail of Holly and her abductor, had literally fallen onto it. It was their trail he'd followed out of the canyon. He could see that now.

Off the boulder again, he searched for a continuation of their trail, and found it with little trouble. He wanted to call out for her, but dared not. He listened for any sound that might expose them in case they were still nearby. Except for a couple of bird warbles, and an increasing wind rustling through the trees, it seemed peacefully quiet.

He was tired, hungry, and weak. He had two protein bars and one beef sandwich left. He needed energy and considered devouring all three. But the sandwich consisted of a substantial amount of beef. He separated the beef from the sandwich and returned it to the backpack along with the protein bars. He then ate what was left—bread, cheese, lettuce, tomatoes, and condiments.

Then, limping, running, walking, and hobbling, he followed the trail for half an hour until he came to a dry wash barren of large trees. At the bottom of the wash, he positioned himself upwind from where he figured they should be, scratched a pit into the soil, and built a fire. With tree branches he fashioned a spit over the flame, removed the beef from his backpack, secured it to the spit, and let it cook.

43

The dampness did not register with Holly until she'd slept for most of two hours in the coolness of the shade, a good hard sleep that she needed. It was the smell of mildew that first aroused her. She could smell the river, her nose drawing closer and closer to the cool, moist dirt that seeped into her mouth. She'd liked the river and lakes in the cool mountains, with tall shade trees that had kept her from turning severely dark from the sun when she was young. It was a time when her parents loved each other, a time when the three of them were family. They would visit the river, she on a blanket with her head in her mother's lap while they watched her father fish. Holly snuggled closer to the dampness. Moist sand collected on her nose and lips. She licked the grittiness from her mouth, tasted its dampness, breathed its humidity.

Then, as if someone had suddenly thrown a switch, her face lit with the revelation of what was there. "Water," she whispered. "Damn, girl, wake up. You've found the river." Her eyes popped open, the tin shed was still at her side, and there was no river. Directly in front of her face, however, was a canteen lying on its side with the top loose, water softly dripping into a puddle on the packed sand at her lips.

Frantically, she pawed at the canteen lid, opened it to its fullest, and allowed the river water to plummet into her open mouth. She did not have to guess or wonder how the canteen got there. She stood up, held it over her head, and slowly promenaded in a complete turn. "Thanks for the water," she half screamed and half cried. "But I'm not going back to the cave with you, you can forget that shit. You're repugnant. You make me sick."

"You are to be mine." An Indian stepped from behind a thicket only a few yards away. "You were brought here for me."

Holly quickly recapped the canteen, careful not to spill a drop, then snatched up a fist-size rock and raised it above her head. She took a defensive stance. "Then come and get me, you son of a—" But the Indian was different. There was no painted face. He was fully dressed, large brimmed hat, denim jeans, shirt, and a jacket, and long braids of hair tied with yellow strings hung at the sides of his face. She recognized the Indian. She had seen him at the saloon and on the streets around town. But that did not matter. She would kill or be killed before she went with him.

In long strides, the Indian moved toward her. She threw the rock. It caught him in the chest and he stopped in his tracks. His head moved one way then the other, and then looked at her. He hesitated for a moment gazing into her stern, defiant eyes. Then he intently scrutinized the woods behind her, as if she wasn't even there.

Though his quirkiness stunned her, she did not take her eyes off him as she slowly leaned over and raked her finger across the dirt for another rock.

The Indian stood post-still, ignoring her. He continued to stare past her, into the sparse forest, as if trying to see through the trees. He leaned sideways, his nostrils flared, his keen senses picking up something from afar, and then he bolted past her.

Dumbfounded, Holly watched the Indian run for a nearby ridge. She looked at the rock in her hand. There was no way she frightened him with the diminutive rock. "What the . . . he's retarded if he thinks I'm going to chase after him," she told herself. Her wide eyes followed him as he disappeared over the crest of the ridge.

She licked her chapped lips, grabbed the canteen, and chased after him. He was the only real person she'd seen since riding away from Troy and Jesse sitting on the porch. And she wasn't even civil to them, she recalled. "Going for a ride, be back later," was about all she'd said. She'd simply ridden off and left them to fend for themselves. "What an ass you are." She chided herself.

She wanted to be home, and if she was ever to see Troy and Jesse again, she had to survive. She would keep her distance, she decided. She would pursue the Indian as he did her. The hunted would become the hunter, and maybe he would lead her out of the forest. But the Indian moved fast and she lost sight of him almost immediately. For several minutes, she stumbled along in the general direction he had gone but soon gave in and crawled beneath a tree. She pulled the canteen between her knees and almost cried again. But she was beyond crying, she decided. The sleep and water had rejuvenated her, she felt much better now and was bitterly determined to endure, one way or another.

She thought about the rock she'd thrown at the Indian. She smiled. It was a damn good throw.

44

Red Hawk ran hard up to the top of the ridge and stopped at the edge of a natural parapet of rocks splitting two winding dry washes that carried rain water from the mountains to the rivers during monsoonal rains. One side of the rocks was a sheer cliff thirty feet above one wash. The other side gradually sloped downward to the second wash. The wind siphoned up from the bottom, bringing an aroma that smelled sweet and harsh at the same time, an aroma of smoke and burning mesquite, of smoldering fat and searing flesh. He had smelled it many times. It always carried with the wind, up slopes and through forests. It penetrated the rocks and vegetation and lingered for hours. As a juvenile, he had followed the scent for miles until he reached various prospectors' camps. There he would watch as the miners devoured cuts of javelina, mule, squirrel, or whatever they had killed and dragged into their camps. Though he had convinced himself that he was a true Indian of the cast of his ancestors, that he could fend for himself, and that he would play havoc on the white man who dared tread on sacred land, he would often wait until the prospectors were gone from their camps or asleep, and help himself to the remnants of their kills.

Red Hawk slipped down the gradual slope, behind undulations of dirt, behind scrubby juniper and sagebrush. And, as if invisible, he came to within a few feet of the searing meat. There, he stopped and crouched behind scrub sage. The policeman Troy was standing in the shade of a clump of palo verde. He wore his police uniform with a pistol strapped to his side.

Red Hawk had tracked the woman Holly from the river. It had been easy, he realized, and believed that Hoskininni had shown him the way, step by step, and he had found her, had given her water, had saved her life.

But the policeman was here to take her away. Red Hawk was aware of that. And he was aware that he would have to stop the policeman without Hoskininni.

He remained perfectly still, held his breath and watched as the policeman looked up into the mountain past him, then north then south, looking but not seeing. The policeman drank from his canteen, stirred the fire, turned the spit, then disappeared back into the shadow of the palo verde. Red Hawk slowly moved, creeping around the thicket until he was directly behind the policeman.

45

Four hours into the match J.C. was down ten to fifteen games, and was getting droopy and careless. His mind was wandering. He stood beside the pool table thinking about Troy and his insistence on going out on his own to look for Holly. And Holly, what the hell had happened to her? Troy had paid the ransom, but still no Holly. Was she dead? That would destroy Troy, at least for a while. Then there was Pike, stabbed by an Indian, one of his own kind for Christ's sake. And then, on top of all of that, Rabbit bopped into town to screw up things, just when everything was coming to order in his life. He was thinking of anything his mind would conjure up but the game before him, the deadly sign of a loser.

But he was getting old and sloppy, slowing down faster than a bug nailing a windshield, one minute tooling along at breakneck speed, then splat. And that's the way he felt, suddenly splattered by life. He plopped down on the chair in the corner of the room, exhaled heavily, and scouted an ashtray for a cigarette butt of smokable size but found none. He tried to clear his mind. He could lean back close his eyes and sleep. He was damn tired and losing big time, losing a game he had to win to insure his happiness for the few remaining years he had left. He had to focus on the game. *You lose focus on the contest, splat it's the windshield for you and you're done for.* He knew that, he'd drummed it into Kid's skull a thousand times, and yet now was failing at such a fundamental. Hang on for at least another hour, he told himself. But he wasn't sure he was up to the task without help. "Hog," he blurted, "I need a shot of Wild Turkey and a cigarette if I'm going to continue."

"No you don't," Hog answered. "You've come way too far to start smokin and drinkin again."

"Don't tell me what I don't need, God damn it," J.C. said snapping the words out. "If you don't go get them for me, I'll hold the game up and get them myself. I need a goddamn break anyway."

"No breaks," Rabbit quickly said. "That's one of your *stipulations* in case you don't remember. But I agree, a drink and a smoke might be just what you need."

"Hog, that's a rule all right," J.C. said. "I can't leave the game, so you'll have to do it."

Hog shrugged, left the room, and reported to all that J.C. was losing badly, not only the game but also probably his mind. Jiffy, the house painter, and a couple of regulars cheered but most groaned.

Five minutes later J.C. was leaning over the table trying to make an impossible cut shot on the three ball when a cup of coffee appeared in front of his face. "Damn it, Hog, what the hell are you doing?" He pulled back on the shot and looked up. Kid was standing beside him holding the cup.

"What the hell are you doing is the question," Kid said.

J.C. stared at Kid for a moment then gave him a big smile.

"I brought coffee." Kid did not return the smile.

"I can see that."

"If you're lucky enough to make the three-ball, then what?"

"I'll run the table."

"No you won't, are you drunk? Look at the table, it's a highly improbable situation, and you should know you're not that good right now."

J.C. scanned the table and realized he had slipped over the edge, far into the loser's abyss, and into what was supposed to happen to his foe. He shook his head and rubbed his eyes. He then slowly and deliberately leaned over the shot, called a safety, and made it.

"What the fuck," Rabbit yelled, "now I have to play both of you?"

J.C. held up his coffee cup and took a sip. "No sissy man, just me," he said and again smiled at Kid. Having Kid here gave him a sudden rush of adrenalin and he was now wide awake and as alert as a jackrabbit.

"I thought about what you told me earlier," Kid said, "and I think you might be right. This game may be your only chance to get mom to stay."

"Am I so unattractive," J.C. asked and laughed, "that your mother would reject me for this hippie freak?"

"Fuck you, you decrepit relic, you fucking has-been," Rabbit said. "She'd dump you for a fucking dog."

"That's my point. She'd be dumping me for a dog."

"I'd bet you a silver dime to a doughnut hole," Kid said ignoring their little outburst, "that you never had to dress up at Halloween."

"Just keep in mind, kiddo. You look just like me."

"Huh uh, I look like uncle Troy, remember? You said so yourself."

"I did, that I did, and it's a good choice you made." J.C. loved the bantering with his son. It made him feel good, and when he felt good he played good.

They both smiled as Rabbit surveyed his shot, mumbled, "lucky bastard," and then took the push-out option by pushing the cue ball to the left with the side of his cue because it was the only choice J.C. had left him. "You couldn't make that shot one in a hundred."

"I only needed the one," J.C. said, then leaned over the table and ran the rest of the rack from there to cut the score to eleven to fifteen. Win or lose, he thought, Kid was back and he felt much better.

46

Troy kept an eye on the campfire; it burned slowly but steadily and the beef cooked gradually. Still he stoked the flames, and cranked the spit. The surface of the meat was charring, but the center still produced plenty of hot dripping fat, which allowed thick smoke to billow and follow the wind.

He stood in the shade and wiped the sweat from his brow. He listened to finches as they hopped from branch to branch and was amazed at the lack of insects— no mosquitoes, no gnats, no flies—and wondered what the birds ate. Mosquitoes and gnats he deplored, and flies, those maggots with wings, were sickening to him, but now he wished for just one to pester him, to keep him occupied, to keep him alert. But he had nothing except the diminutive birds to distract his thoughts, to keep his mind busy. He knew a lethargic mind was just as deadly as a sleeping one, but his head bobbed anyway, and his eyelids had a will of their own, weighed down by long days, rough nights, and a limb-bending tumble down a cliff.

Then something changed. A shift of wind coming from his back, a slight crunch in the packed dirt, the birds were suddenly quiet and the trees seemed still. Slowly, much too slowly, he pulled his pistol, and in the tick of time it took to thumb down the safety a rope flew over his head, past his shoulders, and clenched his arms. It was his rope, taken from his supplies, and he'd heard nothing. He tried to whirl as the rope tightened, pulling his arms excruciatingly close to his sides, and the pistol tumbled to the dirt.

Troy whirled to face Palmer. "What the hell are you doing?"

"You are here to take her away."

"I'm looking for *my wife*."

"She is Navajo, not white. She is to stay with me."

"She is my wife. We have a son named Jesse. Hell, you know that," Troy said, trying to reason with him.

Palmer said nothing, only watched and listened.

"She is my woman," Troy said. "I love her very much and she loves me. She will never be your woman."

"Never?" Palmer questioned. He looked confused.

"If you harm her in any way—"

Palmer continued to stare, processing. "Never," he repeated.

"Never," Troy said, but if you let me go find her, I'll let you—"

"No," Palmer said and the rope pulled tighter and dragged Troy to the ground. Then, flat on his back, he began to move head first up the hill away from the fire and the charred meat.

47

Holly now stood dead still waiting for a ground squirrel to settle in one spot. Then, slowly, she raised her arm high above her head, cocked her hand, and let the rock fly. It was a jagged rock that fit comfortably in her hand. She'd found that she could control that size much better than a larger one, or a smaller one for that matter. The scrawny brown rodent's ears and tail perked straight up as the rock skimmed across its back and hit the dirt with a thud. Then, that fast, the miniature squirrel was gone. "Damn," Holly said, almost relieved that she'd missed, even though she'd convinced herself that she would now eat it, raw if need be—the same kind of animal she'd turned down only a few days earlier—if only she could hit it. She figured killing a rodent was her last hope, and though she'd made several attempts and failed, her aim and throw were getting closer with each effort.

A couple of hours had passed since the Indian had left her the canteen and then scurried away, and the canteen was almost empty. She picked up another rock, bounced it in her hand measuring it for weight and size, rejected it and chose another that felt right. She quietly began walking in the direction the Indian had gone, all the while looking for another critter to appear.

The Indian had told her that she belonged to him, but she didn't understand what that meant. Did he have some kind of hold on her? That's what the Indian in the cave told her, that she belonged to him.

She watched the wind fan the trees and listened to the birds as she tried to sort it out.

Did the Indian take on a different persona when he was in the cave, or was there another Indian? Or, was the other really a phantom, a ghost from the past? Holly believed in ghosts, always had. She'd seen all the television ghost stories and movies, had read the books and heard the stories of evil spirits, and she'd never doubted their existences. But to see one in real life . . . was that possible?

The wind and the birds were the only sounds she heard. She'd given up on the airplane, and the Indian she had chased. She now listened for something eerie, something supernatural, and expected him to appear. But she heard nothing except the wonderful sounds of this beautiful place. It would be a good, peaceful place to die, she thought. But that was yesterday. Today she was going to live.

Then something disturbed her and the hair on the nape of her neck bristled, and goose bumps rose on her arms as a brisk breeze ruffled the trees, and she looked for the ghost. Instead of something sinister, though, the wind carried a pleasant aroma, like her mother grilling burgers early in the evening. The sweet scent filled her senses. She wondered why she was suddenly thinking of the few good times she had as a child, instead of the preponderance of dreadful times. Maybe she really loved her parents and it was getting close to the time for her to make amends and, along with everyone else, forgive them for not being the best possible parents in the world. After all, all parents screw up once in a while when raising their children. She could now certainly attest to that.

The sky, pure blue with cotton clouds in one direction, and dark and ominous billowing thunderclouds in the other, looked surreal. The menacing ones had overtaken much of the north sky. It was going to rain; she'd soon have water and lots of it, but she could use something to eat. She could smell and taste her mother's burgers.

The sun sat high again, past midday but just barely. She could now tell the difference between morning and afternoon, just by watching the sun. In the afternoon, it somehow looked brighter and more yellow, and gave off a more intense heat. The afternoon was usually the hottest part of the day. But today the wind was picking up, carrying the chill of rain with it.

The tree limbs above her head rustled, birds fluttered uneasily from sparse tree to sparse tree, anticipating something, the coming rain probably. But there was something out there—this time her perception was real, not imagined—she could sense it, she could feel it, she could smell it.

Holly sniffed, the aroma was faint; but it was there. Her stomach grumbled. She gathered her meager strength, pulled at anything within grasping reach and groped her way to the top of a nearby ridge. The smell was coming from over the far crest, where the timberline ended and she could see an expanse of washes and ridges. Someone was cooking. A hunter maybe, or a prospector, or it could be the Indian, ghost or not. At this point it simply did not matter. She would have to be cautious, but it simply did not matter.

The smell became stronger, permeated the air, filtering over and around the ridges as she moved from one to another. Then, suddenly it was gone. As the wind whipped in the opposite direction, the beautiful smell disappeared.

"No," she screamed. The fear of losing the smell brought a surge of adrenaline, and she stumbled along the gully, and then clawed up the next ridge. It must be up here. It had to be. This was her last hope, she thought, and tried to control her panic. She cleared the next knoll and tumbled between low scrubby piñon, sagebrush, and palo verde, limbs and thistle smacking at her face and digging into her ragged clothing.

Then she saw it, up the wash in front of a clump of palo verde. "A campfire—" her heart skipped wildly, her stomach churned, and her mouth watered "—something is cooking."

Holly raced toward the campsite. Then she noticed movement at her left and froze rock still. She focused, and a man . . . Troy . . . her husband . . . dressed in his khaki uniform was being dragged head first up the far ridge. A rope lassoed around his shoulders had his arms pinned to his side. And twenty feet above him, at the top of the incline, was the fully clothed Indian, wedged between a tree and boulder, pulling at the rope.

Her mind whirled. Everything was happening so quickly. Frantically she pawed for a rock, her new favorite weapon. The rock had frightened him before, she reasoned, so why not again? She stumbled forward, then stopped. A handgun, lying in the dirt a few feet from the campfire, caught her eye. It was Troy's service pistol. She didn't take time to question the pistol's presence. She simply grabbed it and ran for the Indian yelling, "Hey, you retard, drop the rope."

The Indian stopped, gazed down the slope at her, then continued to pull the rope.

"Shoot, Holly," Troy screamed. "Shoot to kill the mother—"

"Ta-ay!" she screamed as she leveled the pistol. "I am Ta-ay! Look at me!"

The Indian again stopped and stared. He looked perplexed, confused.

Holly squeezed the trigger. The blast startled her but she held onto the pistol.

Tree bark beside the Indian splintered. He flinched, dropped the rope, and staggered sideways.

Holly fired again. This time the shot zinged off the bolder at his side before it went through him. He jerked backwards, turned and leaped over the edge.

Holly rushed up the incline to the top and peered over a sheer cliff. A wide, dry wash wormed its way around boulders and outcroppings of its arid banks some thirty feet below her. The Indian had hit the rocky bottom. She expected to see a cloud of dust mushrooming up from the point of impact of the limp body. But the dust did not rise. The Indian simply hit and stayed put.

"I think he's dead," Holly hollered back. "I think I killed him."

"Are you sure?"

"He's not moving!" she said, then suddenly realized what had just transpired. She ran down the incline and, spent of all energy, collapsed into Troy's arms, sobbing. "My God, Troy. I love you, I love you, I love you," she repeated as she wept and clung onto him.

"I know," he said, rocking her. "I love you too." Troy's eyes also filled with tears.

"And Jesse?" she blurted after a few minutes of crying. "How is he?"

"He's fine. He's with J.C. and his wife."

"J.C. has a wife?"

"Off and on."

"Christ O' Mighty," she said trying to sound like J.C. "I miss him." She began to cry again. "I missed all of you."

Troy laughed. "Yeah, we're family." He picked her up and carried her back to the campfire. "As soon as we get back, I'll send someone up to retrieve Palmer's remains and we'll figure out what happened."

"Who?"

"The guy you just shot."

"Who is he?"

Troy stared at her.

"He's not the one who kidnapped me," Holly said, "if that's what you think. This one saved my life by bringing me water."

"Are you sure? He's the one everyone has been looking for."

"I'm not positive, but the other guy seemed bigger and had war paint on."

"War paint? Face paint, that's what Pike called it. Face paint."

"Black and white bands zigzagging up and down his face."

"So how could you tell it's not the same guy if he had his face covered in paint before?"

"I don't know. He could be the same, I guess. I've been lost and out of it for days, walking in circles, I think, and I only saw the other one a couple of times. But this guy, Palmer, seemed real."

"Real?"

"I don't know, the other one, he seemed so Brigadoon, you know, unaffected by time, like he was from a hundred years ago, like he was a ghost or something."

"Boy, you got it bad. Well I'm not looking for a ghost."

"Who are you looking for, Mister Forkner?" Holly said and hugged him as hard as she could.

"You Missus Forkner."

"Come to rescue me, did you?"

"That was the plan."

"Seems more like I rescued you."

"Never been rescued by a girl before, but am I ever glad you showed up."

"Never rescued anyone before," she said. "So I guess we're even. Are you all right? You look beat up."

"You don't look too hot yourself," Troy answered.

"I am hungry," Holly said and nodded toward the campfire. "I haven't had anything to eat for what seems like a month."

"It's a wonder you're not dead."

"Tonight," she said. "I thought I had died yesterday, but I planned on dying tonight."

Troy tried to smile. "I thought I was dead today too, until you decided to show up."

"I knew you were coming for me," Holly said, heading for the cooked meat.

"How'd you know that?" Troy followed her.

"I saw your plane earlier. I figured you were looking for me."

"That was me alright, but I was looking for Pike," Troy said, smiling.

"Pike? It figures." Holly rolled her eyes.

"Actually, I was looking for you, but then Pike was stabbed by your Indian ghost friend, and I had to fly him out."

"Is he okay?"

"He's in the hospital as sassy as ever."

"Good," Holly said, "I'm glad he's okay. Now what about us, do you know where we are?" She poked a finger at the disintegrated piece of meat as she spoke.

"Probably, but—" Troy took the charred beef from the spit, pulled out his pocket knife, and hacked off a piece of what was now lump of charcoal "—it's several miles and we can't make it today, not with this storm coming in. So let's make the river and get as far down it as we can before dark, then we'll cut around the draw and find the airplane."

"You mean I'll have to spend another night out here?" Holly asked as she tried to force the charcoaled meat into her mouth, then spit it out.

"Afraid so."

"We'll have to find something else to eat, this thing is history." She picked up the chunk of burnt meat and cocked it above her head. "Maybe I can kill something with it."

"Sure. You do that," Troy said. "In the meantime—" he handed her his last two protein bars "—this is all I have left, but we should be home sometime tomorrow."

Holly took the bars and immediately devoured both.

"If there *is* another Indian, he could show up at any time," Troy said as he watched her with amusement. "But, I'll be with you in any case."

"After what I just witnessed, that's supposed to be a comfort?" Holly asked.

"You'd be surprised," Troy said. "Anyway, I was talking about you protecting me."

Holly laughed for the first time in a long while. "I am surprised. I thought I was hallucinating when I first saw you . . . going uphill on the seat of your pants for Christ's sake. How in the world did you manage that?"

"He sneaked up behind me, had the rope over my head before I could do anything about it. I think the cooking meat attracted him."

"I knew it had to be you when I smelled it burning." Holly chuckled. "So I came looking."

"Funny girl. But that's what it was supposed to do. I was pretty sure you would be hungry, but I didn't know you were on your own. How'd you get away from him?"

"I busted him in the balls a day or two ago and ran like hell. He's probably still crying."

216

"Jesus," Troy said. "Do I know you?"

"Actually I caught him right on the end of his dick with my fist and sent him sprawling backwards."

"Christ," Troy said and this time he pulled his knees together.

"I think I shortened it. It was too long anyway," Holly said and laughed.

Troy suddenly looked solemn. "Did he hurt you? I mean . . ."

"No. I'm still a virgin. But it did make me horny." She teased him.

Troy looked relieved. "Everything makes you horny," he said and laughed with her.

They packed up and headed up to the top of the incline where the Indian had fallen.

Holly looked over the edge to show Troy the body. "Shit, he's gone," she said. "I shot him twice but he's still alive?"

"That doesn't make him a ghost. You must have missed."

"Both times?"

"Both times, but maybe you were close enough to scare him into trying suicide."

"Maybe I didn't miss. Maybe he can't be killed and he just fell. Maybe he'll be back."

"Okay," Troy said. "So does that mean you're keeping the pistol?"

"Damn straight," she said and walked past him taking the lead, pistol in hand.

48

It was slow going but Troy and Holly made the river before the sun slid behind the mountain tops. Both ran headlong into the shallow edge of the water splashing, scrubbing at their clothing, and enjoying the freshness of the clear, cold water.

After a short rest, they continued south, where each bend of the river produced a cove of calm water. Troy dug a roll of fishing line and a couple of artificial flies from his emergency kit, and hit each cove by throwing the line in the shallows of the river and then dragging the fly back across the water, at first trying to find a fishing location, and then deciding any bite would do. They figured to eat whatever he caught, fish or otherwise, as he walked along, but they would not stop to "fish." With Holly along, Troy decided to take the longer but easier route around Siphon Draw. Still, if they kept up the pace, they would be halfway to the airplane by dark. But both were getting extremely tired and hungry.

Dragging the line in the water, they followed the river until it doglegged right around a flat, rock-strewn river bank. A litter of gnarled tree branches, driftwood, and river debris covered the area. The topography of the river was as Holly remembered: white-capped water where the river flowed steadily over rocks and around boulders, with a wide, dry riverbed along the bank, and vertical canyon cliffs, void of vegetation and inundated with several natural cavities and caves, above that.

"I know this spot," Holly said and stopped, dead still, then whispered, "This is where the Indian has his cave."

"Are you sure?"

"Damn right I'm sure, I hid right over there." She pointed to a cluster of driftwood.

"And the cave?"

She kept pointing as she turned left and then stopped. "It's in there." She held her arm straight out, indicating that it was behind a stand of trees thirty yards up stream.

The mound of debris at the bottom of the trees looked very much natural, but also somehow out of place. They crept up the river and crawled beneath the rubble. From there they could see the cave's entrance without being seen. Troy motioned for Holly to give him the pistol.

"Now what?" she asked, handing it to him. "There's no way to get to the cave safely."

"We'll do the next best thing," Troy said and then yelled, "Hey, you in the cave."

"What the hell are you doing?" Holly punched him in the ribs.

"Checking to see if anyone is in there," Troy answered.

"Christ, can't we just get the hell out of here, like we have some sense left."

"Not now," Troy said. "I already yelled. You stand guard and I'll go in."

"You're crazy!"

"Scream bloody murder if you see anyone coming," he said as he fished a flashlight from his backpack, turned it on, and started for the cave.

"Idiot," Holly called after him.

He smiled and waved at her as he entered the dark cavern. The flashlight flooded the area with a bright, white glow, creating long shadows along the edges. Slowly, he followed the light through the entrance until it illuminated the whole cave in gloomy black shadows with ominous outcrops here and there. He stayed stooped in a dark corner with his pistol ready until his eyes adjusted. There was no Indian, ghost or otherwise.

The cave appeared pretty much as Holly had described it—a bed of straw-like grass in one corner: a length of rope stretched across the floor, one end tied to a large rock, and a central fire pit in shambles, and stretched across the back wall, a crisscross of stringers hung full of dried slices of jerked meat. Troy fingered the jerky thinking of beef or pork and wondered if it had been salted and seasoned. His stomach rumbled, but he hesitated. He pulled a small slice of the stiff meat from a stringer, wiped it on his pant leg, and popped it into his mouth. It was dry, chewy, and tasted bitterly gamey. He stuck another small piece into his mouth and chewed the tough and rubbery meat as he surveyed the cave, looking for clues to the identity of the person living there. When he found nothing else of real interest, he retrieved another piece of the jerky for Holly.

"When we get back," Troy said when he met Holly outside of the cave, "I'll get some men, come back, and trap him in the cave."

"He'll know you were in there," Holly said. "So he'll pick up and leave."

"Impossible," Troy said. "I didn't bother anything."

"Nothing?"

"Well, I did take a couple pieces of jerky, but there was a ton of it. I don't think he would've counted them. Here, I brought you one."

"Jerky?"

"Yeah, they were stretched across the cave on a stringer."

"Rodent guts," Holly said.

"Rodents? Guts?" Troy made it sound disgusting.

"He tried to feed me one," Holly said. "I think it was a rat or something."

"Rats?"

"He cut them into slivers and ate most of the pieces," Holly said, "but he hung the guts out to dry."

"Oh, crap." Troy grabbed his stomach and belched.

"Probably that too," Holly said. She smiled broadly, twisting her matted hair. "I take it you ate some. Most of it was probably rotted by now."

Troy ran for the river. He began shoveling handfuls of cold water into his mouth.

"You know," Holly said as she followed Troy to the edge of the water, "I'm sure they were all entrails that he used for bait. I'm sure they're not fit for food."

"Entrails, that's the most disgusting thing I've ever heard in my life . . . what the hell does that mean?"

Holly was now laughing. "Entrails, you know, liver, spleen, bowels."

Troy grabbed his stomach again. "But one thing's for sure, all this kind of disproves your ghost theory, because whoever lives in there lives like a human—or an animal—and certainly not a ghost."

"And how does a ghost live?" Holly asked.

"I don't know," Troy said trying to contain his stomach, "but I don't think he would need a bed and food."

"Yum, yum, yum, rodent entrails, that's what I call real food," Holly said.

Troy's stomach heaved. "I'm not really this squeamish," he said, "but that stuff must have really been bad." The thought of spoiled spleens and bowels was all it took and he upchucked chunks of meat that splattered into the river.

"I'll see you downstream," Holly said. She couldn't control her laugher. "You're making me sick."

"You don't know what sick is." Troy hollered after her, and then turned back to the river.

By the time Troy caught up to Holly, towering thunderclouds had moved in, thunder rumbled at a distance, and lightning fired up the clouds, but they paid little attention. They were having a good time amicably needling each other like a couple of school kids as they made headway down the river.

49

Waiting for the nurse to release him, Nina paced the floor around Pike's hospital bed rubbing at her nose. "I don't understand why Troy won't answer his radio unless something's wrong." The hospital had informed her that Pike was being released and that she was listed as his only ride home.

Earlier, Nina had relieved Duke and then spent most of the day driving around town keeping an eye out for Palmer and explaining why she was still driving her wrecked patrol car. "It still runs, and I'm going to drive it until both Troy and Holly are safe at home," she'd declared more than once, as if that made sense. Her short trip to the campgrounds around the reservoir had been a bust, Pike's excursion to the lake damn near got him killed, and Troy had dropped off the face of the earth.

"Troy's a big boy, he can take care of himself," Pike said. "Maybe the radio battery's dead; maybe he lost it, who knows?"

"That's the point, who knows? I have to assume he's lost too, or worse." She'd tried to ignore the *or worse* issue—she'd tried to be philosophical, positive, optimistic like Pike, but she simply couldn't. "I know he's a big boy, but so are you and you got stabbed. And Justman was stabbed . . . and killed, and it wouldn't surprise me if Holly isn't dead by now, too—"

"Calm down," Pike said.

"And if you hadn't had a radio, you'd be dead now. And if something bad happens to Troy—"

"It's not your fault that he's up there," Pike said. "If he still is, and we don't know that for sure."

Nina just stared at him.

"Okay," Pike said. "So he's still up there. But that doesn't make it your fault."

"I know," Nina said. "But why in the hell didn't he report back to us like he was supposed to?"

Pike watched her worry, watched her rub at her nose as she paced. "What's the deal with you and Troy, anyway?" He finally asked what he'd been thinking for some time.

"We have a history, okay," Nina said. She stopped and thought for a moment. "Before he got married."

"Do you still love him?"

"But I can see it's over." She ignored the question. "It's been over for a long time. I guess I kept the flame going far too long because I've yet to find someone that's as good as he is . . . or was."

"Until now," Pike said and grinned.

Nina stared at him and grinned back. "Pike, that's a silly name. Where'd that come from?"

"Hey, I like it. Pike is a spear with a very long shaft."

"Please," Nina said and rolled her eyes. It's a road or something."

224

"It's a long straight road."

"Yeah, right," Nina said and laughed.

"So, tell me," Pike said trying again, "do you still love him?"

"I thought I loved him. We had an on-and-off relationship and the sex was okay, but then Holly came along."

"Sorry," Pike said, then tried to correct himself. "I mean sorry that Holly came along, not about the . . . you know, the other stuff."

"You mean the sex? Are you embarrassed? You are . . . that's so cute. After all that macho stuff about a long shaft, now you're embarrassed. You're just a big ol' good-looking softy. Are you sure you're Navajo?"

"Often I question myself, but I'm pretty sure. Anyway, I can't imagine anyone giving up such a pretty girl as you."

"Pretty, huh? I don't feel so pretty."

"Right, you know you're gorgeous."

Holly looked at him for a moment and studied his eyes. "Boy, you're smooth."

"Not really," Pike said, his smile broadening into a small laugh, "but under different circumstances, maybe."

"A few days ago, I swore you were nothing but a fumble-bum newbie." Holly said. "But now . . ."

"Now what?"

"Well, you are good-looking."

"Are you making a pass at me?"

"No!—" she watched him for a second "—well, maybe just a little."

Pike smiled. "Well, I like you too," he said.

At that moment, thunder rattled the windows and Nina jumped, startled back to reality. She turned to the window and saw a thick, rolling mass of clouds building to the north and moving quickly into the valley. "It's already pouring up along the rim, and it's headed this way with a vengeance. That's all we need, rain and floods to muddy everything up." She paced from one side of the room to the other, stopped, rubbed her nose again, and then spoke in a much calmer voice. "No use sending anyone up there to look for Troy today with this storm bearing down. They wouldn't be able to see anything anyway. But tomorrow I'll get as many men as I can, and we'll start a major search at the lake and head north."

Pike nodded. "Come on, take me home, then you go home and get some rest."

Beautiful man, Nina thought and wondered if he could possibly replace Troy in her heart. He was right about one thing, though, she was tired, and wanted to go home. A hot bath and good night's sleep would do wonders for her weary body.

Outside, thunder reverberated through the valley as the ever-increasing black clouds blotted out the moon.

50

Red Hawk stood tall and broad atop a rampart. One of the ricocheting bullets from the woman Holly's pistol had grazed the side of his head weakening his sense of equilibrium. The rushing wind from the pending storm swirled viciously around him, pushing hard against his wide form, whipping his blood-tangled hair up and away from his dreary face. Still, precariously at the outer edge of the vertical cliff, he kept an unyielding balance. Except for the fifty-foot drop, nothing stood between him and the couple at the bottom. Red Hawk watched them trudge across the rocky riverbed as they followed the river south. He watched as they jostled, talked, and laughed. She looked weak and weary in her tattered clothing, struggling through the sandy soil and rocky riverbed, but still pleased and happy to be with him.

"Never," Red Hawk said. He envied the policeman. He wanted to be desired by the woman. He could see it. He could feel it. He could hear her heart beat, the sound amplifying with each up rushing gust of wind. Her heart beat not for him, but for the white man, and Red Hawk wanted to bellow out and let all know of his anguish.

He watched them both, but only saw her. His head filled with passion. He had never known a woman in that way. None had ever wanted him. They would back off, stammering with excuses. Though he saw himself as tall and archaically handsome, he knew most whites and all women saw him as ugly and repulsive. Twice in a distant past he had grabbed a girl off a dark Flagstaff side street and hauled her into the forest with the intent of having her. But when each looked at his face and began to cry and beg him to let them go, he let them go. They rejected him so he rejected them. His white mother had instilled the belief that all women and their wishes were to be respected, no matter what. He simply could not force himself on them.

This woman Holly had shot him, had rejected him for the white policeman, as she did Hoskininni. If Hoskininni could not keep her, how could he?

With that realization, the regrets of his life whirred within his head. The self-doubts, the insecurities of his youth again began to creep into his psyche. He was a person who should never have been born. He always knew that, but never wanted to admit it. He was hideous, an ugly red man with a white man's name.

Mark Palmer.

He hated the name and hated himself for having it. He hated his white parents for giving it to him. He hated his real parents for creating him. He hated his own people for thinking of him as an outcast, someone from the past, someone to be discarded and forgotten. And he hated Hoskininni who had failed him. He had learned the ways of the Navajo Witchery Way and had called

Hoskininni to help him be brave, to help him with her. But it did not happen.

Palmer now knew she would never be his. And through eyes filled with tears, he gazed upon her from afar as she ambled away from him, her beautiful Indian face darkened by the sun. He reached for her, stretching over the cliff's edge, grabbing at her tiny form, and yearning for her to come to him. He wanted her to be the mother of his children. An erection throbbed and pushed against his trousers. But now she was fading away.

Tears ran freely and Palmer grabbed his firm penis, pulled it from his trousers, and pointed it skyward.

"Fuck you, Hoskininni. Fuck you spirits and gods. You have all failed me. I will never call upon you again."

He jerked, yanked, and pulled at his erection. It grew hard and strong, swelled larger and larger until the explosion came and spewed into the air, streamed far out, over the precipice into the firmament that belonged to the gods of his people and the spirits of his ancestors.

Palmer fell to his knees. She would *never* belong to him.

51

In the sixth and final hour of the match, J.C. had made a miraculous comeback. They were now tied at twenty games each and J.C., with all the confidence in the world, was bearing down on the last shot, a combination eight-ball into the nine-ball for the win. His stroke was smooth and dead on and the cue ball hit the eight-ball with precision, but the eight-ball bobbled when it hit a miniscule scuff in the billiard cloth. An abrasion of normally small consequence, but this time the eight-ball wobbled and caught the nine-ball ever so slightly off-center and skewed it into the jaws of the corner pocket. It hit the edge of one cushion facing, bounced to the other side of the pocket, and stopped less than a sixteenth of an inch—a few fibers of worn-out billiard cloth—from going in.

J.C. stared. The nine-ball sat there staring back at him. Moisture collected in the corner of his eyes, and he raised the cue up, ready to strike it over a rail, break it into a million pieces. But he stopped and simply laid it softly onto the table. "Good game," he said to Rabbit, turned, and walked from the room.

"Of course it was a good game, you old dick-wad," Rabbit called after him. "I knew you'd blow it. You don't have the balls to win either Nine Ball or Blondie."

Jiffy was standing just outside of the doorway. "Yahoo," he yelled, raised his hands, and pranced about. "He lost. The old, decrepit son of a bitch lost. I knew damn well he would." He was out the front door to spread the word and collect his winnings. He had bet against J.C. many times in the past, but this time it had paid off. It had paid off big time.

Rabbit turned to Kid.

"Rack 'em," Kid said.

"You break," Rabbit said, grinning. "It'll be the only shot you get."

Kid made the six-ball on the break then ran eight straight balls for the win. He tucked his father's Rambow under his arm, let it hang shotgun style, and walked out of the room.

52

Nina pulled what was left of her cruiser beneath the overhang of the cottonwood tree where Pike usually parked his Corvette just as the rain let loose. The drive from the Upland Medical Center to Pike's cabin had taken several minutes, which were spent sharing some of their pasts and their hopes for the future with each other.

Pike looked through the cracked windshield at the deluge driving hard through the canopy of the tree. "I hope someone had the good sense to put the top up on my Vette before *she* left it at the lake," Pike said.

"Hmmm," Nina said. "Sorry."

"It'll be a bitch trying to get it out of there, but I'll—"

Nina stared at him.

"What?"

"Listen, I . . . it's been interesting taking care of you at the hospital, and I—"

"Hey, I know. You want to go home, right?"

"Right."

"But you don't expect me to make it into the house by myself, do you? After all, they had to haul me out of the hospital in a wheelchair."

"That's standard procedure," Nina said and laughed. "They bring everyone out in a wheelchair."

"But in my case, I need help, not to mention that it's now raining bullets. What if I slip and break something? Wouldn't you feel bad?"

"Yeah, come on, invalid." Nina rolled her eyes and kicked her cruiser's door open. "I suppose I can help you inside."

She supported him as he crawled out of the car and unsteadily moved up the slippery flagstone sidewalk. He was leaning heavily on her.

"You're being a big baby."

"Am not, I need help."

"You need help all right."

By the time she safely guided him through the front door of the cabin they were drenched. She stood at the open door, wind and rain blowing past her as she took in the neatness of the small cozy room. An overstuffed leather sofa with coffee table, and matching recliner with side table, positioned on a Native American style rug, were all facing a rock fireplace. There was no television. "Nice." She sounded surprised.

"It's messy. I would've straightened it up, if I'd known you were coming." Pike closed the door behind them. Then, trying to look somewhat helpless, he shuffled toward the kitchen area. "You're soaked. You need a good cup of hot tea before you leave."

"Tea, huh?" she said. "Got any wine instead?"

Pike already had the teapot in his hand and almost dropped it, thinking of the implication. "It's Navajo tea. My mother's recipe, it'll warm you up and take all your inhibitions away at the same time. It's magical, much, much better than wine."

"Maybe I want my inhibitions." She was now shivering and dripping on the wooden floor. "Do you have any dry clothes I can borrow?"

"I have a flannel shirt and warm-up pants in the closet. No undies, though."

Nina smiled at his use of the word undies. "And no pajamas either, I assume."

"Never use them."

"Whatever you have will do."

"I'll get them."

"Never mind, I'll find them. You fix the tea. It sounds good." She turned toward the bedroom.

A few minutes later he heard the shower running. "*Náshidít 'įįh*," he said as he poured two cups of tea and set them on the coffee table. He had thought about suggesting the sweat lodge to warm them, but now figured a slow burning log in the fireplace would do just as well.

When she came out of the bedroom wearing only his shirt and warm-ups, with nothing on under them he was sure, his knees went weak. Her hair, wrapped in a towel, rose above her clean and clear face. "Jesus," he repeated, this time in English, then add, "Wow."

Nina grinned. "Don't get any ideas, newbie. I just didn't want to catch a cold. But since I'm here, I am hungry."

Pike pointed to the refrigerator but said nothing.

"I'll fix us something. You go put on some dry clothes before you get pneumonia on top of everything else."

When Pike came out of the bedroom wearing an open shirt and gray baggy workout pants, Nina's hair was no longer in a towel but now fell in more than a few pencil curls to her shoulders.

"Looks good," Pike said.

Nina smiled. "You don't have any real food, but I came up with something to nibble on."

This time Pike smiled. He wanted to comment on the nibble statement but held his tongue.

As the storm raged outside and the fireplace heated the cabin, they savored two cups of Navajo tea while snacking on thinly sliced mutton, goat's cheese, and wheat crackers.

He could smell her clean skin, clean hair, and natural clean fragrance. On her, his shirt was loose-fitting but the shadowy points of her pert breasts were unmistakable. She was thin but toned. Her full, moist mouth and sensual brown eyes tugged at his heart, his mind, his trepidation, and he leaned in and kissed her lightly on the lips. Her mouth opened a little. It was warm and sweet from the tea. He slid his hand under her hair to the back of her neck; pulled her closer and kissed her harder.

She returned the kiss, long and passionate.

They held their embrace for a whole minute, kissing and giving in to the warmth of each other. Then they parted.

"What time is it?' she asked.

"Does it matter?"

She sat for a long moment and did not take her eyes from his. "No," she finally said and then leaned in and kissed him again. She used both hands, one behind his head and the other behind his back.

He did the same. Her tongue was warm and quick, her skin on fire. He slid his hand under her shirt. Felt her hand pushing his shirt off his shoulders. Felt her nails against his arms.

"I don't usually do this," she mumbled. "Not with people I work with."

"We're not working."

"What are we doing?"

"I'm an invalid, remember. You're taking care of me."

"That's for sure," she said and raised her arms high and held the pose until he pulled her shirt over her head and ever so tenderly kissed her breasts, one then the other. She held him there for a moment then spread her fingers wide on his smooth broad chest and pushed him slowly backward. She ran her fingers down, past the bandages around his stomach, and undid the cord holding his trousers.

Several minutes later, they were naked on his bed, locked together with her on top, making love, at first with a kind of patience and tenderness he had never experienced before. Then as her tempo increased, he matched her stroke for stroke, thrust for thrust, with a fury that he had only hoped to someday see in her, feel with her, be consumed in with her. All he wanted to do was lay there on his back and come at her with the same enthusiasm she was showing him.

"Jesus," he said when she finally collapsed at his side.

"Sorry," she whispered. "It's been awhile and I got carried away. I hope I didn't hurt you."

"I think I'm going to die, but who cares?"

She laughed. "I care," she said as she snuggled in his arms, and was soon snoring.

"All natural," he said to himself and smiled.

53

As the rain began, Troy and Holly left the expanse of the river looking for anything that would provide adequate shelter. In a narrow alcove at the base of a dry wash, well away from the river, they made a quick camp. A slab of overhanging rock that jutted from the cliff-like bank protected the alcove not only from the weather but also from anyone coming from any direction except straight in.

At first they'd decided against a fire, but sopping wet and sure they were going to be there for a while, they changed their minds. Troy gathered scraps of wood, and watched Holly's every move as she built the fire against the whirling wind. She'd lost a few pounds, was beat up with bruises, cuts, scraps, and had wild matted hair, but was nonetheless very sexy in the way she moved. The round bottom he'd watched sail over the corral fence was still there.

"So, why were you walking in circles?" he asked, trying to get his mind off his typical male thoughts. "Why didn't you just stay on the river instead of going up the mountain?" He added a couple pieces of wood to her fire.

"I was trying to get away from the Indian ghost or crazy Indian or whatever the hell he is, but then I got lost and confused."

"You are talking metaphorically, right? Tell me you don't really believe he's a ghost."

"He was pretty frightening when he attacked me, and like I said, he looked like he came from a hundred years ago. And he shifted, you know, from one spot to another. I'd always heard about Indian spirits or ghosts when I was a kid in Montana. So, yeah, I guess I do believe in them."

"He shifted? You mean he moved?"

"No, he didn't exactly move. It was like he was here—" Holly pointed in one direction than another "— then he was there. One second he was right beside me and the next, he was on the other side of the cave."

"Uh huh," Troy said. "Fear can do strange things to your perceptions. Or you were simply dreaming."

"Frightened is not even close, I was terrified. And it did seem to always happen just when I was waking up."

"There you go then. So I think we can eliminate your ghost theory. I think it was Palmer and if he's still alive we're well ahead of him."

"I hope you're right."

"Come on. Let's try to get some sleep so we can walk out of here tomorrow."

They curled around each other, close to the small smoldering campfire and, feeling warm and somewhat safe, Holly was fast asleep.

Troy, however, tossed with worry. He had nothing to worry about if Palmer was injured in the fall.

But if Palmer wasn't severely hurt, he'd be fast on their trail. More importantly, what if there was another Indian, a coconspirator of some kind maybe—someone bigger and faster, someone who hid behind a painted face? The odds of having two crazy Indians running amuck in the same forest would be astronomical. But, what if there was another? Would he be ready? Not knowing what else to do, he double checked the load in his pistol to insure that it was dry.

Though the overhanging slab protected them from most of the storm, the rain was now coming in at a bounding slant, driven by gale-force winds. Thunder and lighting, barreling down from the north, raged, and was getting stronger by the minute.

And Troy noticed the water starting to flow freely down the wash.

54

As Holly slept, she snuggled close to Troy. It felt good to have her in his arms and he had a hard time letting go, but the rising water wasn't looking good. When he shook Holly's arm to wake her, she came up swinging.

"Hey, hey, it's me, Troy," he said, defending the blows with his arms.

"Shit," she hollered, "you scared the hell out of me."

"Sorry, I'll not do that again."

"Damn right you won't. Just remember, I have the gun."

"Noted," Troy said and laughed, and decided it wasn't a good time to tell her that he actually had the pistol. "You missed breakfast."

"Really, what did you have?"

"Scrambled eggs, bacon, and coffee."

"Funny man," she said, and he heard her stomach rumble.

"Truth is the storm's coming pretty fast so we need to hurry."

They hastily packed their gear and started down the wash. Rain was bombarding them now that they weren't protected by the alcove, and they quickly found themselves knee-deep in rushing water.

"This isn't going to work," Troy hollered over the noise. "The storm's worse than I thought. We have to get out of here."

"Which way?" Holly could see the water swelling and gaining speed.

"Let's forget the wash and go straight up toward the top of the cliff . . . the water's coming in too fast for anything else. If we try to follow the wash to the river we may get trapped." Troy tied a rope between them, secured his backpack, and started climbing.

The earth rumbled with a sudden, deafening roar.

"Earthquake?" Holly hollered over the clamor, clinging to a jetty of rock.

"Climb," Troy screamed as he led the way. "Climb!"

"Cyclone?"

"Flash flood," he yelled over the uproar. "Now go . . . go."

The gushing water pouring over the side of the rock face made ascending even the simplest terrain strenuous, but Holly climbed behind Troy, pulling her way up the rocky slope until she made it twenty feet up the steep precipice. Large, fierce raindrops pounded at their skin as Troy forced himself over the rim and onto the relatively flat mesa.

"Climb, Holly," Troy yelled at her. But her hands could no longer hold her and she tumbled backward into the rolling water.

242

55

J.C. straddled a stool at the bar and demanded a shot of Wild Turkey from Dana.

"You don't need it," Hog said. He was standing behind the bar with Dana.

"Ain't going to happen," Dana said. "Not from me."

"You don't understand, I've lost everything," J.C. said.

"So you lost a miserable pool game," Hog said. "Big deal. You've done that before."

"If Blondie leaves you," Dana said, "you never had her to begin with."

J.C. got up, poured himself two fingers of Wild Turkey and sat back down in front of it.

"You do whatever the hell you want," Hog said, "we got work to do." He and Dana walked away.

J.C. stared into the glass and allowed the aroma to drift up into his nostrils. He loved the smell of good Kentucky whiskey, it was what had attracted him to it in the first place. It was a reason for drinking; a reason for living, and it was powerful.

"So, you imbecile, you played pool using me as the stakes and Rabbit beat you. You should be ashamed of yourself."

Kid and Blondie were now standing behind him. Blondie held Jesse in her arms. "Ashamed of using you?" J.C. asked without looking up. "Or ashamed of losing to that hippie piece of shit?"

"Both, I guess. But mostly for letting him beat you."

"He didn't beat me. I lost. There's a difference."

"So there is," Blondie said shaking her head. "But it's the same results. And you've certainly helped me to make up my mind about what I want to do."

"No doubt," J.C. said and sighed.

"Not the first one you ever lost, won't be the last," Kid said. "And mom's right, you *certainly* should be ashamed of yourself."

J.C. eyeballed his son. "Humph," he said and thought about implicating the boy for helping him with his rogue game, but let it slide. "Maybe I should've let you play him."

"Maybe you should have," Kid said.

"So, the way I understand it," Blondie said, "now I get to leave with Rabbit without interference from you or your big, bad brother."

"Humph," J.C. said again. He picked up the shot of whiskey, sloshed it around, took a whiff, savored the aroma, and sat it back down.

Blondie handed the baby to J.C., picked up the Rambow, and disappeared into the pool table room.

Kid started to follow her but J.C. stopped him. "This is between your mother and Rabbit, son. Let them have their space, and don't try to stop her. I was the idiot that played the game."

Kid sat at the bar with his father, but kept his eye on the door his mother had just walked through. "I told you, I'd go with her. And I meant it."

"Can't blame you, son." J.C. said, trying to balance Jesse on his knee and gaze into the glass of whiskey at the same time.

A few minutes later, Blondie came out still carrying the Rambow.

"I didn't hear any pool playing," Kid said looking at the cue.

"Protection," Blondie said, "I only took it for protection."

"Protection?" J.C. and Kid said in unison.

"In case Rabbit couldn't handle rejection." She smiled, her round eyes glistened.

J.C. slid his hand behind his back and Kid gave it a smack, kind of an underhanded high-five.

"I have no intentions of going anywhere with him," she said. "I've caused you two enough grief and heartaches in your lifetimes, and if it's okay with you guys I'd like to stay right here and help raise my son like I'm supposed to, and baby Jessie if need be."

"Fantastic!" Kid hollered and hugged his mother.

Dana and Hog looked up from pretending to be busy at the far end of the bar, smiled, and gave J.C. a thumbs up.

"Saddle up," J.C. said to Blondie while tapping the stool beside him, "and I'll buy you a drink." He pushed the whiskey glass aside. "Three Cokes, Dana, the Forkner family is thirsty."

56

The wind's ferocious force sucked at him, trying desperately to dislodge Troy from his perch. He planted his feet at the edge of the mesa, braced against unsecured rocks, and pulled at the rope tied around Holly's waist. Holly came bobbing out of the turmoil taking in more water than air but managing to grab the rope to right herself. But the wind and water pulled hard against her and she added nothing to help Troy as he continued his losing battle of halting the drag of her dead weight.

"Pull, Holly. Pull at the rope," Troy screamed into the wind trying madly to coerce her into helping. But she went under then bobbed up then went under again and appeared to be doing all she could simply to hang on.

The rope burnt into Troy's hands and his feet slipped in the muck, dislodging one rock after another. He was so close to the edge that he would have to abandon the rope, jump into the chaos, and hold her above water until she reached shore, if he could get to her in time. Tit for tat, he thought, his life for hers. It was his fault she was out here so the only way for redemption was to jump in before she went under for good. Then, at the instant before he leaped, the rope tugged backward and his forward slide halted. Troy glanced over his shoulder to see a wild-looking Palmer wedged behind a boulder pulling the rope.

Troy said nothing. The help gave him renewed hope and energy and he pulled harder. With Palmer doing most of the work they strained, one hand over the other, until Holly slid from the water and onto the muddy slope.

She came out limp and still. Troy straddled her and began mouth-to-mouth breathing to force air into her lungs, and stomach pressure to force water out of them.

He continued, breathing and pressure, back and forth, breathing and pressure, until suddenly she gasped, expelling a mouthful of water and inhaling a mouthful of air. She came up coughing with her eyes open and fixed on Troy's.

"Jesus," she said and locked her arms around him and began to sob like a baby.

As Troy held Holly tight to his chest, he kept a keen eye on Palmer. He had no doubt that Palmer's sole purpose in helping was to save Holly, and now that she was out of the water and breathing, he had no idea what Palmer would do. Palmer, however, just stood as fixed as a weather-beaten statue, bent slightly forward against the wind, swaying neither forward nor backward.

***

Palmer was as static as a rock, not because of the hard, cold rain, but frozen by the whirlwind of contradictions in his mind. Standing not six feet from them, he had watched the white policeman work frantically but expertly to save her.

Palmer watched them as he moved closer. Nothing was stopping him. He could grab the policeman and fling him into the rage of the water. He could pick up a rock and smash it into his head first so there would be no struggle. The policeman would be dead, gone, out of the way.

But if he killed the policeman, he would have to kill her also because she would *never* be his.

And as Holly coughed back to life, with her arms around Troy, Palmer turned and walked towards the churning water.

***

Ever mindful of Palmer standing behind him, Troy held onto Holly. They stayed locked together in the mud and pounding rain until a roaring, pulsating sound brought them back to reality, and Troy tried to ease his hold on her.

"This time you saved my ass," Holly said holding him tight. She made no effort to let go.

"I didn't do it alone," Troy said and motioned upward. But Palmer was moving and, lit up by a rapid burst of lightning, they were just in time to see him leap headfirst into a monstrous wave of water. The wave bore down the wash ruthlessly driving toward the river. Palmer went under without a struggle.

But also coming down the river, among the debris, a water-logged coyote swam with long graceful strides, as if running in tall grass, and, parallel to where Palmer had gone under, the coyote also plunged beneath the waves.

248

"Come on. We need shelter," Troy said pulling Holly to her feet. The storm had reached its full force, lightning flashed, thunder rumbled, and water streamed across the ground contributing to the ever increasing flow of what now seemed like a river at their feet.

They quickly crawled to the lee side of a boulder and huddled, only slightly protected from the howling wind and bombarding rain. Visibility was limited but Troy could make out boulders of various sizes, scrub vegetation, and little else. He was about to move forward when a flash of lightning stopped him. He motioned for Holly to stay put.

"What is it?"

"Quiet," he whispered. "I thought I saw something moving, another coyote maybe. But bigger."

"Another one?"

"It could be the same one that was in the water, I guess. I don't know. The damn things are everywhere."

Holly stood dead still, squinting into the rain. "There," she whispered. "Did you see that?"

Troy watched her, said nothing, but strained to see in the direction she was indicating.

"Look—" she pointed "—something moved, from left to right. But it didn't exactly move. It shifted from one place to the other."

Troy pulled the pistol. "I didn't see anything."

"It's gone," Holly said. "It was there a second ago, now I don't see anything." Then, "there—" she kept her voice low "—rounding that large boulder. It is the coyote, but standing upright like a man."

When Troy did not respond, "there," she whispered again, "by the boulder."

More lightning flashed, and when Troy looked toward the boulder he saw not a coyote but a naked Indian, with the physique of a weightlifter, standing tall. The strobe lightning made his painted face appear shredded, like an orange being peeled, against the black background. The Indian was searching. He didn't know where they were. The boulder hid them from his field of vision.

"What the hell?" Troy said, still whispering.

"That's him. I told you he's not from this time," Holly said, trying to mouth the words without making noise. "That's the one who held me captive."

"He sure as hell don't look much like Palmer in that getup," Troy said.

"Why would Palmer help you drag me out of the water then come up here looking like that?"

"He wants you alive," Troy said, "but me dead."

"That's not Palmer," Holly insisted. "This one looks like the rock drawing I saw earlier in the canyon above us. I think this one is a ghost or something."

"Don't let you imagination go crazy, Holly. If he's not Palmer then he's just some other wacko."

"I'm telling you, he's a ghost or something," Holly said, still whispering. "And he only wants me if I'm willing."

"Why would a *ghost* want you?"

"Because I'm friggin awesome."

Troy tried to laugh but couldn't. "So, if he's a ghost, I can run up to him and he'll disappear?"

"Don't be crazy, he'll kill you."

"What if I shoot him?"

"He'll still kill you."

"So what do we do?"

"Wait until he's gone then get the hell out of here."

"I think he's just your run-of-the-mill crazy person named Palmer."

"I think he's a ghost and he killed Palmer for helping us and if he can't find us, he'll disappear again."

"Well, whatever the hell else he is, or might be, he's a kidnapper and a killer and he needs to be taken in, and that's my job."

"No, he doesn't and no, it's not," Holly said. "Let's just stay hidden, right here, and wait until he leaves."

But the Indian turned and headed for them.

"Too late," Troy said. "I think he heard us."

"Ta-ay?" The words came from the Indian but sounded as if they were coming from within a deep barrel and barely audible over the drumming rain. "My woman, Ta-ay."

"Shit," Holly said watching the Indian.

Troy raised the pistol but the Indian instantly slid behind another bolder. "I can't get a clear shot."

"You better be right," Holly said.

"About what?"

"About him being just another fucking crazy person who wants me alive." She stood and moved several paces to Troy's left. "Yes," she yelled at the Indian and waved her arms, "I am Ta-ay."

"My woman, Ta-ay." The voice echoed from behind the tall rocks. Then the Indian was suddenly in front of her, his hands reaching out.

251

Troy, though astounded by the swiftness of the Indian, realized that Holly had exposed herself to harm and possible death to give him a target. He had to make his shot count. He steadied the pistol with both hands, took careful aim, and squeezed the trigger.

The shot struck the Indian's torso. His mouth dropped open and he emitted a deep growl that sounded almost like a laugh. He turned toward Troy and pulled his knife; its stainless blade sparkled and the fangs of the bizarre snake's head handle shimmered from the backdrop of continuous lightning.

"Ta-ay!" Holly screamed. "Look at me, you son of a bitch! I am Ta-ay, your woman Ta-ay." Lightning flashed, this time big and bold, lighting up her perfect form, and rain saturated her dark hair, making it long and straight.

Sighting at the silhouette of the Indian's ragged head, Troy pulled the trigger again. "Ghost, my ass," Troy said and the pistol roared.

But again the shot did little to faze the Indian. He raised the knife high above his head and threw it.

Troy fired another round as the knife slammed the side his head, taking a swath of hair and a piece of his right ear. But this time the pistol's blast seemed quiet, almost nonexistent as thunder boomed across the canyons, and lightning illuminated the mesa to the full glare of day. The seemingly impotent shot, however, bore into the Indian's left eye and burrowed deep into his skull, finally finding something vulnerable. His yowl came loud as he turned and rushed Troy.

Troy, now on his knees, stood his ground and took careful aim. This shot penetrated the side of the

Indian's head. He yelped then howled like a mad dog, but he kept moving, seized the pistol from Troy's hand, and flung it aside. Troy went stumbling after it but the Indian's fist caught him full in the face. Troy tumbled backward and the Indian was instantly standing over him.

Holly retrieved the pistol and held it close to the Indian's head. "I am TA-AY," she said loud and clear, announcing each syllable separately and plainly. "Do you want me, you ugly fuck?"

The Indian stopped and turned toward her, his foot hovering above Troy's chest. "Ta-ay?" His head tilted well left as he peered from only one eye. "Ta-ay." This time his voice sounded human, almost normal, pleading even. He did not resist. He did not flinch. His cycloptic face merely stared at her.

Point-blank, Holly fired the last bullet. It splattered the garish eye.

"Lights out," Holly said.

The Indian pawed at his head and stumbled backwards but did not fall.

Troy came up with the knife, jumped onto the Indian's back and forced it solidly into his chest. The Indian seized Troy by an arm and a leg, heaved him high into the air, and sent him sprawling into the mud.

Not hampered by the loss of sight, the Indian picked up a hundred pound boulder, hoisted it over his head, and aimed it at Troy. Again, the sky became as bright as day. Blue lines of lightning ripped through the air. A massive bolt struck the boulder and seared down through the brutish Indian, instantly turning him into an unrecognizable molten mass with fireballs erupting into the ground.

Then there was darkness. The putrid smell of burning flesh permeated the air as vapors rose from his torso. The mass that was once the Indian staggered in expanding circles until he reached the mesa's rim and leaped over.

Troy and Holly watched as the dehumanized form vanished into the churning water. Troy pushed himself to his feet, hobbled to the edge, but could see only trees, logs, branches, and other churning rubble tumbling down from far north. Holly joined him, held his hand, and they watched as the lightning faded, and the thunder eased into a gentle but study rumbling as the fury of the storm subsided. Troy shivered. "I wonder?" he said.

"It's the spirits," Holly answered.

"Do you think he's dead?"

"If he is, we didn't do it."

57

This was one of Nina's favorite times while living in northern Arizona, the day after a major thunderstorm. She sat on Pike's back stoop sipping a steaming cup of coffee. Overlooking the vast tree-studded valley below, she could see for miles and certainly understood why Pike had chosen this land. The sky was bright and clear with a few billowing clouds lingering high above the mountains, and the air, though still moist, had a clean, refreshing feel to it, like a rebirth of the atmosphere. She had not planned on sleeping as long as she did, but Pike and his tea had swept her off her feet—literally, she smiled at the thought—and Pike had let her sleep well into midmorning. She had the best night's sleep she'd had in months.

She finished her coffee and, reluctantly, forced herself back into the house where Pike's breakfast was awaiting her. "Not bad," she said looking at a table set to perfection—eggs, bacon, toast, and more coffee. "Something I recognize."

"I aim to please."

"Yes you do."

"Now what am I supposed to do, kiss you?" Pike asked.

"You'd better, if you know what's good for you."

He wrapped his arm around her waist, pulled her tight, and kissed her long and passionately.

"Back off, pervert—" she pushed him away and laughed "—just a kiss."

"Pervert?"

"You do have a picture of me by your bed."

"I don't lie." He pulled her close for another kiss.

She returned the kiss then broke away again. "We're already late for work."

"I'm convalescing."

"You can convalesce at the office. After last night, I think you have more than enough stamina to get some work done. And we have a lot to do."

Pike complained a little, but after breakfast he quickly dressed in a clean uniform then followed Nina, in rumpled but dry clothing, back to the wrecked cruiser.

They bypassed the new construction and drove straight to the old station. There were three vehicles in the graveled parking lot: Duke's cruiser, Joe's beat-up old sedan, and a cruiser in a space marked CHIEF.

"See if the keys are in it," Nina said pointing to the odd cruiser. "We'll borrow it this afternoon."

While Pike checked out the vehicle, Nina walked into the station wearing the rumbled, and once again wet uniform, thanks to a rain-soaked car seat of her cruiser. Both Duke and Joe had been pulling double duty and gawked at her as if she were alien. She rubbed at her nose. Something was amiss. She could feel it as soon as she opened the door.

"Got caught in the storm," she said explaining her uniform, and smiled awkwardly.

They stared at each other then back at Nina.

"How's Pike?" Duke asked.

"He's coming behind me," she answered.

"I'll bet," Duke said and gave Joe a high-five, and they laughed like school kids.

"All right, wise guys. Act like grownups."

Both clammed up to a snicker when Pike walked in.

"What?" Pike grinned and winked at them.

"Don't you encourage them," Nina said. "They're already acting like idiots on their own. They don't need your help."

With that, Pike's grin stretched across his face.

"Any word on Troy?" Nina asked ignoring the tirade. "Or do we have to start rounding up another search party?"

"Yep," Duke said, "they're at the hospital."

"What?"

"And both are okay," Joe added. "Apparently Troy found Holly a-wanderin around in the forest, and they flew out in Troy's plane early this very mornin. They've been there for a couple a hours . . . and they don't want no one to disturb 'em for a while, so don't you go a bustin in down there."

Nina looked at the front door, thought about it for a second, thought about bolting, but didn't. "I can understand that," she said, "but what I don't understand is why no one cared to tell me they were here."

"We tried to get you at the hospital," Duke said. "They told us that Pike was released to you yesterday.

We tried your radio but you were apparently too busy to answer it. And, since Pike has no phone . . ." he shrugged.

Nina frowned. "And they're okay, that's good news."

"Beat up, but good as gold," Joe said.

"Was Holly alone when Troy found her?" Pike asked.

"Apparently not," Duke answered, "but Troy said they shot the guy several times."

"No shit?" Nina said. "Unbelievable. And I missed the whole thing."

"Yeah, if you spent as much time being a cop as you did being a private nurse, you'd be on top of it," Duke said.

"I'd bet my horse to a pig in a poke that she was on top all right," Joe said and they both laughed again.

Nina ignored the two old guys. "But what about the Indian Troy shot; did Troy say who it was?"

"No, but the sheriff's department pulled that Palmer fella from the reservoir this mornin, stiff as a board, and beat up pretty bad." Joe said. "Some never-come-home campers saw him floatin down a wash. Looks like he was caught up in a flash flood and drowned his self, but Troy don't know about that yet."

"Drowned? I thought you said Troy shot him."

"We don't have an oh-ficial autopsy yet," Joe answered, "but Troy never said who he shot."

"Christ." Nina again fiddled with her nose. "What else did I miss?"

"They're having a fallen officer's parade at Window Rock tomorrow afternoon." Duke answered.

"What?"

"Deputy Justman's funeral is in a day or so," Joe said. "They're a-givin him a hero's sendoff tomorrow for dyin in the line of duty while recoverin the ransom money. Ain't that a kick in the ass?"

"I can't get my mind around that one," Nina said. "Justman? A hero? What the hell? It's a kick all right."

"Why is it happening so fast?" Pike asked. "Shouldn't they wait until the case is closed?"

"It's closed," Joe said. "I'm tired of bein here round the clock, all the time."

"But there's more," Duke added. "You want to talk about fast. Silverwood is having an estate sale. Everything Justman owned will be auctioned off the day after the funeral."

"That scumbag," Nina said. "Silverwood doesn't have anything I want. And neither did Justman."

"I don't know," Pike said. "Some of his artifacts are priceless. I'm thinking we should bid on them and take them back to the Hualapai where they belong."

Everyone looked at him and he shrugged. "Just a thought."

Nina plopped down behind her desk. "In any case, I'm glad it's over, I'm glad Holly's home, and I'm happy for her and Troy—" she looked at Pike, rubbed her nose, and smiled "—I'm finally, truly happy for them." Then she hopped up and headed for the door. "Come on, newbie; let's go back to the hospital."

"Hey," Joe protested.

But they were already out the door.

58

After several drafts and rewrites, Troy finally hit upon a version of a report that he and Holy could both live with. "Are you sure this is what you want to do?" he asked.

"Yes," Holly said. "I was delusional most of the time. When you're lost in the wilderness, tired, hungry, and beat up, irrational thoughts tend to take over your mind, you see things that aren't there and then start to believe them to be true. I saw crazy stuff, the White Rabbit's house, a coyote standing on its hind legs, an Indian moving without moving, stuff no sane person would admit to seeing, and I certainly don't want any of that mentioned in any report. Everyone would think I was the crazy one."

They were sitting on an old leather couch in the doctor's lounge at the hospital with baby Jesse asleep in a portable crib within arms length of Holly. They were finishing the report that they had verbally started on the long trudge around Siphon Draw to the airplane, which had taken most of the night. They then refined it a bit during the short flight back to the airport and the drive to the station where Duke called an ambulance and sent them to the hospital. They even discussed it while the hospital emergency staff did their jobs with sutures and bandages. They had even collaborated with J.C. when, at Holly's insistence, he and Blondie brought Jesse to her. The report would be simple and to the point, they all agreed, nothing outside the realm of possibilities.

"Okay then," Troy said after listening to Holly make sense once again. "We've made this as palatable as we can without going into great detail. So let's make it official and go home."

Holly wrapped her arms around him, gave him a long and passionate kiss. "I can't wait to be at home with just you and Jesse. I missed you guys so much and will always love you."

"I love you so much," Troy whispered and returned her hug, powerful but gentle.

They were about to leave when Nina and Pike strolled in.

"Good timing," Troy said and handed Nina a manila folder. "File this report for me, and we'll call this ordeal over, we're going home . . ." he trailed off when he saw Nina's uniform, pulled the folder back and handed it to Pike.

"Got caught in the storm," Nina said defending herself again, then snatched the folder from Pike. "Couldn't this wait until later?"

"We wanted to get it done while we agreed on everything that happened," Troy answered.

"And what would that be?" Pike asked looking dubious.

"Palmer attacked us twice," Troy said. "Once dressed as himself and once dressed as an Indian with a painted face. We shot at him several times on both occasions. The second time did him in, and he fell into the water. I also believe that it was Palmer who stabbed you. And Duke told us that Justman was killed recovering the ransom money. I also believe Palmer killed him too. It's all in the report. You guys can read it if you want, but that's our account."

"The sheriff's department pulled Palmer's body from the reservoir earlier this morning," Pike said, "and Doctor Miller, in one of his many capacities at the hospital, examined the body. He determined that the cause of death was drowning, apparently caught in a flash flood."

"We know," Troy said. "Doctor Miller told us an hour or so ago, but that's not official and so doesn't change anything anyway."

"There were only bullet fragment wounds," Pike said, "none of which would have killed him, according to Doctor Miller."

Troy glanced at Holly. "The only thing we can tell you is that we shot at him at least six or seven times. Maybe we missed in all the excitement, I don't know. But, whether it was the bullets or Mother Nature that killed him is of no consequence to us."

Pike scanned the report, hitting on the highlighted statements. "So, you're saying the big painted Indian and Palmer were one and the same."

"That's our story."

Pike looked at Nina.

"Beats the hell out of your skin crawler theory," Nina said. "But Palmer could have had an accomplice and that's the Indian Troy and Holly actually shot."

"That's a possibility," Troy said. "We'll wait and see if another body shows up. In the meantime Holly and I will stick to our report. It was one guy, Palmer, and we shot him, or at least at him."

"They're Skinwalkers," Pike said matter-of-factly. Then turned to Holly, "Were there any coyotes around?"

Holly glanced toward Troy. "Coyotes? Arizona is full of coyotes, what are you talking about?" She stepped close to Troy and held his hand for support.

"Never mind," Pike said. "It was a bunch of Navajo stuff I was thinking about, but nothing I want to pursue right now. You guys are probably right anyway."

"So, now that that's settled," Troy quickly spoke up, "I think we should all go down to the morgue, identify the body, and be done with it."

The town morgue was a small refrigerated basement room of the hospital, accessed by a stainless steel-clad elevator barely big enough for a gurney, so Doctor Miller led the gang down the stairs and into the small cold room.

There were no drawers or specific container for the deceased. Palmer was simply laid out on a gurney and covered with a white sheet.

"Now what?" Holly asked as everyone gathered around Palmer's gurney.

Doctor Miller pulled the sheet from Palmer's head.

Holly studied the pale fractured face. It was disfigured beyond recognition. She shook her head and closed her eyes. "I . . . I don't know."

"Pike, you saw his face," Troy said. "Take a look."

Pike bent over Palmer's head. "Man, he's chewed up pretty bad. It's hard to tell. And he was painted from the neck up. And it was dark. So it's hard to tell—" Pike watched Troy, then Holly "—but, yeah, I'll agree that this could be the Indian who attacked me."

"Well I got a good look," Troy said, "and I think that's him."

"There's only one way for me to find out for sure," Holly said regaining her composure. Slowly and carefully, she pulled the sheet down past his genitals. She grimaced, closed her eyes again, and shook her head negatively but answered, "Yes, it's him. I'm sure of it."

"Just like that?" Pike asked. "One look at his junk—"

"It's him," Holly said firmly.

Pike elbowed Nina and smiled. "Would you recognize me by my—" he stopped and looked at his toes when Dr. Miller gave him a hard stare.

59

In the twilight that evening, Holly relaxed on the back porch, enjoying her third glass of Pinot Noir. She leaned far back in her chair, a la Troy, with feet propped up on the railing. She had ridden Chance around the arena for a few laps, fed her, and put her in a stall for the night. Troy had taken Jesse inside for bed time while she now mellowed and collected her thoughts.

She was glad to be relaxing at home, finally, without interruptions and without a gaggle of other people around her. And now, without doubt or reservation, she knew this was home. Troy and Jesse were family. This was *her* home and *her* family, and she loved them very much. She and Troy had spent a couple of hours simply being close, holding each other, and playing with Jesse, affirming there love and commitment to one another. Sex was never discussed or necessary for that affirmation. The closeness of each to the other was all that was needed.

She smiled contently, emptied her wine glass, stretched clumsily to pour another drink from the bottle resting on the railing, and then settled back to her sitting position.

The wind seemed unusually still considering the rage of yesterday's storm. Except for the pain of a healing stab wound and various other cuts, welts, and bruises to remind her, the last few days now seemed surreal, almost like a distant past, or something she had imagined. She sipped the red wine and let it rest briefly on her tongue before she swallowed. She loved wine the way Troy loved beer. But that's okay, she thought, a drink now and again to settle the nerves is probably a good thing.

But visions of the mangled mess that was Mark Palmer laying on the gurney haunted her. The body was so distorted it was a wonder that anyone could even identify him, and she was supposed to say that he was not only Mark Palmer, but also some demented Indian with a painted face. And that's what she had said because she didn't want to cause Troy the embarrassment of having a crazy wife, one who saw phantoms and ghosts.

But she knew what she saw and would never forget it. It simply was not physically possible that they were one and the same.

She listened to a couple of woodpeckers getting their last meal for the evening, and a pair of distant lonely owls, courting she guessed. She looked out over the back lot. The serenity and beauty was overwhelming as her eyes followed the trail she and Chance had taken many times. Wild red roses, columbine, and deer's ear stood tall and still while their colors faded into the darkness toward the forest. She was enjoying the beauty of it all when abruptly, at the fringe between daylight and darkness, a man-sized coyote materialize. It appeared from the obscurity of the dark woods into the twilight of the field, stopped, set back on its haunches, and stared at her, as a tame obedient dog would.

Holly sat mesmerized.

After a moment, the coyote howled, a long and sorrowful cry, and then slowly dissolved into the darkness.

Holly had no misgivings. She knew he was still out there yearning for her.

Made in the USA
San Bernardino, CA
06 September 2015